Praise for Ray LeCara Jr
and
FROM WHERE I SIT

JANUARY 2023 LITERARY TITAN
GOLD BOOK AWARD
WINNER

"Well-written. Well-crafted. Each story examine[s] different areas of the human condition and the emotional aspects of life."

Literary Titan

"An engaging collection of stories about life, love, friendship, family, and more. This collection of compelling narratives may provide some answers to one of the most difficult questions everyone eventually faces regarding the meaning of life."

Reader's Favorite

Also by
Ray LeCara Jr

Future Destiny

When Worlds Collide

The Forgotten Prophecy

*Of Space & Time: A Collection
of Science Fiction Short Stories*

*Dark Awakenings: A Collection
of Haunting Short Stories*

*Essential Study Skills:
A Holistic Approach to Learning*

*Who Are You, Really?
The Search for Authenticity*

*Best Foot Forward:
A Student Success Guide with Life Skills
Strategies for the Road Ahead*

FROM WHERE I SIT

A COLLECTION OF SHORT FICTION

RAY LECARA JR

SEATTLE

Published in the U.S. by Syner-G Publishing, Seattle.

Publisher's Cataloging-in-Publication Data
Names: LeCara, Ray Jr, author.
Title: From Where I Sit: A Collection of Short Fiction / Ray LeCara Jr.
Description: Seattle, WA: Syner-G Publishing, 2022. | Summary: From Ray LeCara Jr, a five-story collection of thoughtful, diverse, character-driven short stories. Three tales about choice and consequence with compelling narratives that remain with the reader long after the stories are read and two that find characters confronting their mortality in exotic locales. From Where I Sit: A Collection of Short Fiction is a gripping page-turning literary experience.
Identifiers: LCCN: 2022914157 | ISBN: 978-1-7379394-4-3
Subjects: LCSH Short stories, American. | BISAC FICTION / Short Stories (single author)
Classification: PS3612.E222 F76 2022 | DDC 813.6—dc23

Book Jacket Images and Design © SGP | Scent of Juniper image c/o Macaskill Wright | Pixabay/StarGladeVintage, Gorkhs, Michael Hourigan, Albrecht Fietz, Amy (PrettySleepy) | All other interior images licensed under Creative Commons Zero 1.0 Public Domain License

Printed in the United States of America

Syner-GPublishing.com

First Edition

To Dianne...

For your friendship, your continued support, and engaging conversations. Always thought provoking. Always a pleasure.

"Death is not sad. The sad thing is most people don't live at all."

–Dan Millman

Dan Millman is the author of *Way of the Peaceful Warrior: A Book That Changes Lives*

Stories

SCENT OF JUNIPER 01
A WWI agent confronts his greatest foe.

A LIFE LOST LIVING 13
A college student finds a mentor he
didn't realize he needed.

GOLDIE 41
Finding happiness sometimes requires
trusting your instincts and stepping outside
your comfort zone.

ONE NIGHT IN BANGKOK 81
Knowing who to trust can mean the
difference between life and death.

OLD LANG SYNE 87
A woman confronts her past
when she bumps into a former lover
on New Year's Eve.

SCENT OF JUNIPER

The mercenary's steel blue eyes were attuned to every movement. Having just completed a successful mission tracking down a rogue agent, recent intel brought Burr here to the city of Gdynia in search of a rare, fabled Renaissance Fabergé egg. Arriving in Poland a mere two days following the signing of the Molotov-Ribbentrop Pact, a non-aggression agreement secretly signed between Germany and Russia, possession of the egg meant access to possible classified intelligence relating to the treaty. That is, if the intel received checked out. And if the egg actually existed.

Blending in, Burr helped himself to a glass of wine from a passing waiter. Admiring the delectable buffet lavishly displayed on the finest of linens, he sipped his wine stepping under high archways separating the massive rooms of the castle's hall — architecture originating from the second period of the Renaissance. Above him, in addition to the great many burning torches, grand chandeliers illuminated cathedral ceilings of lacquered gold accented with lavender tapestries that hung from the large open arched windows. The castle, a massive structure spanning several thousand square feet, was closed off except for the hall and garden area off to the side of the main building. Abutting high-rising cliffs set against the Baltic Sea, the castle overlooked the Gulf of Gdańsk. If the Germans were planning to invade, it was difficult to imagine when so easily distracted by the surrounding beauty.

Deftly, Burr made his way through the aristocratic crowd that reeked of alcohol and opulence. Noblemen and politicians engaged in haughty conversations while their mistresses in backless, tapered evening gowns giggled and drank the night away. They all gestured and flirted, signaling private messages under a smoky haze suspended overhead in a giant white cloud. Even the few who wore large gowns ballooning from under their monstrous bosoms were having no problems finding attention.

Tonight's dinner party featured some of Europe's elite, not just Poland's upper echelon. Among them, Burr recognized the aging, yet decorated British military hero, General Fargus. A veteran of the First World War, the general also fought against Turkish rebels in the Turkish War of Independence until a skirmish on the battlefield nearly took his life, sidelining him for the remainder of the war. An aged but hideous scar obscured by a bushy white mustache were among the many visible reminders of his glory days. Anxious to return to military duty, he was among the small contingent of British personnel assigned to advise the Polish Army during the Polish-Soviet War. It was during this time that he acquired a great many influential friends.

Now, several years later, the world, especially Europe, was once again in turmoil. Former Polish prime ministers and politicians alike were keen to hear the general's opinions on matters of a growing Nazi state. The air was ripe for another worldwide conflict, bigger than even the first. Yet you'd never think it so by watching him tonight, laughing and enjoying the young ladies on each arm.

Burr wondered if anyone in the crowd knew the truth about the general's son. Purportedly the leader of a well-financed underground group of militants — Nazi sympathizers — Renford Fargus was becoming a thorn in the side of governments worldwide. Their goal: infiltrate and eliminate the military elite of designated countries, thus contributing to the success of any Nazi Germany pact or invasion. This put Renford in direct odds with his own father, a military hero, no less.

Burr came across Renford once before, just weeks earlier. But he miscalculated Renford's moves. What a coincidence, then, that he should receive word the egg would be here in the same place as the general. Could this mean

Renford was here also? Something about the whole scene smelled foul. Surely if Renford was anywhere near as ruthless as his father was in his youth, there was nothing stopping him from assassinating the general — his own father, and the man advising the Polish military on German affairs.

A flurry of activity occurred about Burr, enveloping him in a familiar scent. As he inhaled the fragrance, it elicited memories of a past relationship. An unhealthy torrid affair. Careful to avoid eye contact, he intently scoured the crowd to identify the source.

Ascending the white marble spiral staircase to the right, a figure distracted Burr from his reverie. Pausing, once he pivoted to look over the crowd, Burr realized it was Renford. Emptying the contents of his glass in one swallow, Burr placed it on the flat surface of an abstract stone sculpture before making his way up the stairs feeling for the steel beneath his black jacket.

Atop the stairs he ventured right. Listening for voices, he gently checked for unlocked doors. The vaulted hallway, extending nearly as far the eye could see, was adorned with a narrow carpet of plush burgundy. Most of the heavy wooden doors with latches were locked. Burr's muscles tensed as he suspected a trap outside the one door that was slightly ajar. Stealthily he entered the dark room, hands tightly gripping his Walther PPK.

A pop echoed from downstairs. Gunshots. Then several more. Attention diverted momentarily, Burr strained to pick up anything useful from the disturbance below. Shouts and screams were all he heard until the large wooden door was violently slammed into him, trapping his hand in his jacket.

Over and again the door struck Burr until he fell into the hallway. Ignoring the pain in his shoulders, he lifted his feet over his head somersaulting to an upright position. Removing the semiautomatic pistol from his pocket with one hand, he unfastened the single button on his jacket with the other and kicked open the door. Quickly stepping aside, he anticipated a shot that never came. There was only the sound of balcony doors rattling as the wind pulled them open and closed.

Guests ran through the corridor, panicking in response to the commotion in the hall below. Burr cocked his pistol. Sweat glistened his forehead. He held his breath as he approached the balcony. Renford may have slipped through his fingers, but he was surely still on the grounds.

Burr swiftly searched the dark room. His mission to retrieve a priceless egg allegedly used to pass along German military secrets was now in jeopardy. The only one in existence dating back to the time of the Renaissance, it was smaller than the eggs produced by the House of Fabergé. Crafted during the end of the

Renaissance in France, it was the work of Karl
Fabergé's great, great grandfather. It would take
moving from France to Germany and then to
Russia, nearly three generations later, before
the family began crafting the eggs again. Allied
control of this egg and its secrets could provide
an advantage over the Germans. But seeing
Renford and the general here only complicated
things.

Frustrated that he came up empty, Burr
returned to the staircase. Descending a few
stairs, he assessed the situation. Someone was
yelling orders in German. Amid the crowd, he
could see the general alive but bloodied. Guests
bumbled about. Some fanned themselves, tipsy,
and oddly complacent, as if they were enjoying
a day at the theatre.

A woman in the crowd screamed. She
pointed upwards. But not at Burr. Burr whirled
to meet the approaching assailant bearing a
German made Walther P38. The aggressor
barely had a moment to raise his hand. For Burr,
there was no hesitation. He fired one shot. In
the time it took to blink, the target had already
found its home between the attacker's eyes.

Burr glanced over his shoulder quickly
enough to catch two more armed men heading
for the stairs. With a head start, he retreated to
the room he inspected earlier. There, hidden in
the darkness, he planned to remain invisible
until it was too late for his attackers. He kept

the door ajar. Waiting. Ready to lure in the assassins.

A frightened woman emerged running and shrieking from the other end of the carpeted passageway. She was met by a barrage of bullets as the two assassins opened fire. The sound of gunfire boomed through the cavernous hallway. Again, Burr did not hesitate. Given the window of opportunity, he stealthily emerged from the darkness. Eyesight aligned with his right arm, Burr concentrated on his targets. In one fluid motion he genuflected just as he fired three successive shots. The first shot terminated the assassin on the right, tunneling a hole into his forehead. A bloody opening appeared just slightly above the left eyebrow. The other two shots found each of the knees of the assassin to the left.

Astride his would-be executioner, Burr stuffed the hit man's mouth with a handkerchief to stop the coward's bellowing. With his pistol to the man's temple, he sought the answer to the number of assassins on the premises. While he hoped his seriousness had been demonstrated by his excellent marksmanship, it was not to be the case. The man held up only one shaky finger. There was little time for games and no mercy for liars. Standing, Burr finished off the hired gun with one final shot — executioner style.

Certain the other assassins would expect him to descend the stairs, Burr braved a ten-foot jump from the wrought latticed balcony of the unlocked bedroom. Landing on a narrow walkway of stone above a three-hundred-foot drop to tumultuous waters below, every step brought him closer to death. He shuffled gingerly to the great hall's verandah.

Through elaborately paned glass, he evaluated his adversaries. One shooter stood by the stairs. Another by the general, gleefully bludgeoning him with the butt of a weapon. There was also a killer in the middle of the crowd. But instead of keeping watch, he was more interested in the young ladies.

Burr took out the general's attacker first as he entered from the verandah. Gurgling erupted from the assassin's throat while he collapsed into a growing pool of crimson. Shards of stone pelted Burr's skin as bullets followed his dive behind a pillar. Executing a roll Burr came up on one knee, aimed his pistol, and fired a shot that greeted its target. The last assassin — surrounded by a bevy of beauties — met Burr's glance. Fumbling, he never had a chance. Burr was ready. Without pause he fired the one shot that was needed.

Giving a sweep of the room, Burr holstered his pistol. He moved quickly to attend to the badly wounded general knowing it was imperative he get him to safety.

"How many?" Burr asked the general.

"Five. Perhaps more." The general's eyes fluttered, remaining open only with effort. "My... my son?"

Burr wasn't sure where Renford was. He certainly wasn't among those dead. Not yet anyway. "I don't know."

Though General Fargus struggled to breathe, he managed to pull Burr close. Having also taken a wound to the chest, the general was lucky to still be alive. His face was swollen and bruised. "Beware... Fire Flower... The agent... She knows!"

"It's okay," Burr soothed trying to comfort the old man. Turning to the people in the crowd. "I need a coat. Something for the general's head. Now!"

Vulnerable, Burr's guard was down too long as he tended to the injured military man. Time was running out.

But as Burr wrestled with his next move, the general went limp in his arms following the echo of another pop. Pistol in hand, Burr whirled about. His nostrils flared as he searched the cowering crowd, pointing his weapon at every suspicious looking character. That is, until the scent of juniper seduced him.

From within the parting crowd, she emerged with her own pistol drawn. Any other time, Burr wouldn't have faltered. Yet here she was. The woman from Burr's past. He should have known when he picked up on it earlier.

Bright hazel eyes pierced his own blues. Drowning him with her intoxicating scent, she drew closer. Her cheek brushed his and he felt her warm breath on his ear. "I'll take that if you don't mind."

Unable to do little else, his eyes closed as the woman's treasonous lips found his.

And then she was gone.

The sound of a motorcar echoed in her wake. Burr made it outside just in time to catch a shadowy glimpse of Renford and the juniper woman.

Burr was beside himself. For the first time in his life, he wavered. The cost, as he was about to find out, was greater than he could have ever imagined.

A LIFE LOST LIVING

I watched Old Man Maguire — that's what he went by — step painfully out of his beat-up green Ford pickup. It was a relic. Like him. Supporting thick, poorly circulated legs, his booted feet crunched the frozen, stiff leaves beneath him. Leaning against the pickup, he swallowed back a Yukon Jack nip and deeply inhaled.

He had been talking about this place for the longest time. Since the summer when I first met him. Since I began working at the restaurant to earn spending money for school. My first year of college. First time away from home.

"I was born on a lot not far from your school," he shared that evening in August when I first met him. He was pretty relaxed sipping at his Jack Daniels, his second favorite to Yukon Jack. "Of course, back then the area wasn't nearly developed or as densely populated as it is now."

At the time I was a busboy. My shift was over and we got to talking. Old Man Maguire was an enigma, though. People knew of him but didn't really know him. He seemed to have so much to say about everything. Seemed to know everything there was to know about things. Yet there he sat nearly every night. At the bar. Alone. Too often drinking until he was wasted.

Some nearly seventy years ago Old Man Franklin Maguire was born in a bucolic part of Connecticut not far from where I was attending university. Sibling to five brothers and one sister, he grew up working on his father's small-town New England farm.

"That's a big family," I told him. It came as a shock until I recalled my mom was one of three and my father was one of seven. Me? It was just my brother and me. I was the oldest.

Old Man Maguire, Frank, slowly waved his hand dismissing my comment. The speed, gesture, and minimal words were his *tell* when he was over his limit. I still wonder to this day how he ever got home some nights.

During another conversation he shared that larger families were necessary if they were farmers. Everyone was expected to pitch in once they were old enough to start walking.

Life was hard then from what he described. But since life was much simpler, he reasoned that's how families somehow managed to survive. For Old Man Maguire, that was until his father died. Frank was quite young at the time.

"Died of a heart attack right there on the field." The old man's voice was barely above a whisper that night around Labor Day. He was staring into his fourth glass of Yukon Jack when he disclosed that personal bit of family history.

Later that evening he revealed he was the one who found his dad, though I was provided various versions of the story in the days that followed depending on the number of drinks he had in him at the time.

After Frank's father passed, his mom tried to hold up the family as best she could only to lose the farm because it didn't generate enough income. With her oldest sons off fighting Germany and Japan, there was no one left to tend the farm. A strong but diminutive woman, she couldn't do it herself. Not with young children who needed tending. Not with a daughter who succumbed to a rare breakout of measles. And it was too expensive to hire help.

While Frank never saw combat in World War II, he did fight in the Korean War. Lucky enough to make it out of one of the most destructive conflicts of the time, his two older brothers did not.

"It was tough. The mood changed so quickly after the second war. There was so much loss but there was a sense of... People felt like we had done something good, you know. Such arrogance. I don't know that we ever got over the Korean War."

I shared my knowledge of it but thought it was just as devastating what was done in the previous war and in Vietnam. None of it made much sense to me. But I wasn't a military brat.

My dad was in the Vietnam War, but we never talked much about the military or about military engagements. When we did it was very generalized. Topics only touched the surface.

Frank didn't respond to my comments. Instead, he finished his recollections about how soon after returning stateside he married, reiterating how there were so few things to feel good about.

Maguire's eyes did light up when he talked about building a house not far from the family farm. It meant he'd always be close to his mother — the heart and soul of the family. When his two younger brothers moved out west, however, they took their mother with them.

"Where'd they move to?" I asked.

It took him a moment to recall. "Colorado. Longmont, Colorado."

"You never visited?"

Frank shrugged. "Too busy. The family rarely spoke, so..."

His mother died about twenty years ago. Asleep in her bed. At Frank's brother's house. The old man wasn't even told until after the funeral.

"I'm sorry," I told the glassy-eyed man. I don't know that he ever registered my words of sympathy. He just looked straight ahead, his head bobbing slightly. At the time I thought he fell asleep with his eyes open. But I know now he was reliving memories long since passed.

That was the way things went when he was younger. The family had grown apart, embittered by the loss of family members and their father. His was a generation of repressed anger and hostility. No one communicated until issues boiled over to the point where the family's only way to express emotion was to argue. Explode in pockets of rage that left a mark even when apologies where offered.

After losing the farm, Maguire's mom began losing her strength and eventually her faculties. The final straw was receiving news of her sons' death. It didn't matter how brave or heroic the tragedy. After her husband, it was the loss of her children that broke her. Until then, Frank remarked, his mom was the strongest one of the family. Even if she was probably keeping up appearances for her children.

"And after?" I inquired.

He tipped back the glass to empty the last drop onto his tongue before answering. "There were moments of lucidity, but she was never the same."

When speaking to Old Man Maguire before his liquid medication took hold, he was a force to be reckoned with. Either because of — or in spite of — his earlier experiences, Frank knew what he wanted in life. He just always had to navigate his demons to get it.

Serving his country, for example, was a choice — one that he did proudly. He was determined to go no matter what. He also viewed it as a tribute — a tribute to his father who served in World War I and to his older brothers who served in World War II. Once discharged, he determined himself to marry his sweetheart from high school. Though, again, given the night of recollections, other versions seem to exist regarding the early days of his marriage.

One such story was nearly ripe for the movies. It is, as one would imagine, the version he told on Veteran's Day. His high school sweetheart, Elizabeth, was waiting for him with open arms when he came home from the war. Ready to start their lives anew, he claimed they couldn't get married fast enough.

Another version, perhaps more truthful, was that Beth thought he had died along with his brothers. Got the story mixed up somehow and was dating a guy they both knew from high school. Once Frank found out, he beat the shit out of the new boyfriend. Guess the guy used to be a close friend. Heavy on the *used to*. Kind of Maguire's modus operandi I've come to learn. At that point Elizabeth didn't have much of a choice *but* to marry her former flame.

Still another version was that Elizabeth became pregnant shortly after Maguire returned home. And at that time, there weren't many options. So they did the responsible thing and married before the child was born.

I never did ask him to clarify which version was the accurate one. Sometimes I was treated to a version that was a combination of all three.

Following the marriage of his sweetheart, he attended college and went on to become an accountant. He always worked hard for what he wanted and never shied away from a challenge.

Back in the woods on a cold January morning, Old Man Maguire surveyed the familiar terrain before us. He pointed out the now overgrown area where he and his wife made their home. Remains of a house that burned to the ground near a large lake that was clearly beautiful no matter the time of year.

"Check out the way the snow sits along the edges there," he said as we began walking through the overgrowth. "I always thought that was so beautiful."

Walking as best as he could, Frank made his large frame over to where the foundation was, squinting to catch a glimpse of the lake beyond the firs and leafless trees. The lake was the one constant here since Frank's childhood. His conversations nearly always returned to it. I understood now why he was so set on building here. The farm that he grew up on down the street may no longer exist — its long since abandoned buildings sold off most recently to land developers — and his own house here reduced to ash, but the lake remained. It was his playground as a child and his place of solace as an adult.

Reaching into his shirt pocket, hidden under the overalls, Old Man Maguire found his Marlboros and lighter. Lifting a cigarette to his lips, his right hand flipped open the lid of a lighter belonging to his dad. He paused for a moment, thoughtfully rubbing his thumb over the inscription that bore his father's name: Flint Maguire. Then systematically, as I've watched him do countless times at the bar, he flicked the chamber with his thumb to ignite the flame. Maguire lit his cigarette and inhaled the nicotine before parking it to the side of his mouth.

He told me in December how he was directed by his doctors to quit. The self-made man was oblivious to such requests. He lived life by his own terms. He was determined to die on his own terms.

But failing to heed the warnings only worsened the circulation, limiting his ability to walk or even move at times. His smoking, along with the diabetes that was discovered some five or six years ago, only aggravated the circulation in his lower extremities.

Restricted to doing less and at half the speed, this was no more evident than after a few drinks when gone was his strength to move about from the bar stool to the bathroom. On nights I was working and noticed it was bad, I called him a cab.

Deteriorating, Old Man Maguire's body was defeated. His blue toes reminded him of that every morning. But his head of hair — wisps of gray — was combed to perfection just like when he was a teenager. I think he was still putting grease in it.

Shadowed slightly by the day's growth of stubble, his haggard facial features were a crisscross of intersecting highways that revealed a life of labor and struggle. His shoulders sagged, as one might come to expect for someone his age. I gathered it was also the heavily weighed bitter memories.

"Penny for your thoughts?" I asked beginning to get cold. I was never a fan of New England winters. Still not a fan. To me, they last way too long, but I was out here because it was important to the old man.

We were standing near the foundation of his former home. He was lost in his thoughts, sucking away on his cigarette with intensity.

He spat off to his left. "It's something, you know?"

"What is?"

"How we were raised on a shoestring. Don't know if we'd have made it in this day and age."

"Seems the big guy upstairs was watching out for you."

He shot a rare cold glance in my direction. It meant I was talking out of my ass.

"You're kidding right? Kids growing up without a father. Brothers dying in a war. The horrors we witnessed during our tours. The smells. The sounds. They don't go away. How is a man supposed to live after an experience like that?"

The question was rhetorical. It wasn't my place to answer since he also didn't seem finished.

"We were never much of a church-going family," Old Man Maguire explained. "There's never been a god to me now or when I was younger. What I do remember of God was my dad and his belt. Those are my earliest, *my only*, memories of my father. Beyond that belt was whatever code you came face-to-face with on the playground or in life. Discovering. Learning. Believing. But only through experience. Only through the hard knocks of life."

I looked down and kicked at the snow. "I'm sorry."

In getting to know Frank Maguire, I learned that he was a man haunted by his war experiences even to this day. This was, after all, the generation that was dropped off after they returned without any real regard for their mental health and the witnessed horrors they could never forget. Making matters worse, it took generations to acknowledge how so many vets dealt with long forgotten memories in their older years. Memories that often returned with a vengeance.

It didn't help that everything in his life had been an uphill battle. It's why he questioned the existence of a god. No such god would allow a man to bear so much misery for so great a time.

At every turn.

At every chance there was to be happy.

His eyes darted for a moment. Then I caught it too. Followed the patches of purple, blue, and green. Two little kids we saw up the road earlier in the hour, both looking around eight or nine, were sprinting about. It was so quiet here their laughter was easy to hear. They were with their parents — who looked like kids themselves — when Frank waved to them.

Maguire was looking around. And I knew why. "Wonder where the parents are?" I asked.

"We probably just can't see them," he replied. I'm not sure if he was dismissing any worrisome thoughts on my account.

"Safer in the woods, though, than in the road," I fished.

Frank knelt on one knee to take some of the pressure off his more painful leg. The knee made an impression in the clump of snow beneath him. Hearing the children I know made him think of his own. There was something in his facial expression just then. A memory, perhaps. Guilt.

"Only if you're respectful of the danger," he replied. "Mother Nature can be cruel. The ice may not be hard enough."

"Speaking from experience, are ya?"

"Oh, yeah. It can be deceiving." A wave of guilt creased the lines on his face. Maguire noted his failure as a parent. His failure to properly prepare them for the future by teaching them things they needed to know to survive a harsh and cruel world. "But I was always working."

"What's that?" I asked.

He shook his head to clear the thoughts. "Lotta memories out here."

I nodded. "Imagine so."

"Problem with life is there is so little time for much else..."

"You think so?"

It was around Thanksgiving when we started to have longer interactions. Stressed out about school, my parents, my girlfriend. Life. I needed someone to vent to. I just didn't know it at the time. Frank needed someone too. Someone to whom he could impart the wisdom of his years. Wisdom borne of his mistakes.

"You're young yet but when you're working to get ahead, there are only so many hours in the day. Something's gotta give. And between work, the kids, the marriage, the mortgage, it's one damn crisis after another." He spit into the wind. "Shit! Suddenly the kids are all grown up. Old enough to move out, they leave. Never to return. Never to call back."

He was right about that. Before today, he spoke glowingly about his kids. Around New Year's he let slip his daughter, now twice married with three of his only grandsons, lived over in Colorado close to the uncles. They barely spoke and he hadn't seen her in years.

Slurring his speech as he sobbed into his nightly dosage, he lamented why she never called. "I don't know what I did. I don't know if she's angry with me. Or why!"

"Have you ever asked?"

"She won't ever call me back."

Working missionaries, his son, a priest, spent much of his time in some of the more devastated and remote parts of Africa. Up until only this year Maguire didn't know that. He just knew that his son, Mason, named after Frank's father's middle name, went off to join the seminary. He didn't even come back when his mom was sick.

Frank inhaled as he acknowledged his failure as a son and exhaled in his recognition of failure at being a father.

"Did I ever tell you the doctors refused to acknowledge my wife's claims? So they never followed through with the proper investigative care."

"Why was that?"

"They were convinced my Meredith was merely suffering severe bouts of fatigue and depression. Only when it was too late to operate did they discover the tumor."

Old Man Maguire's eyes were distant again. "Her death was a long, drawn-out painful experience."

"I am so sorry."

He looked at me, his eyebrows angled upwards with a pained look in his eyes. "And I bitterly cursed her for it."

What I had come to learn was that Frank was never as happy as he was when he was a young child playing around the lake before his father passed away. Yet those memories seemed too distant to ever recall with much clarity. As he grew older, he resented the sorrow that always overshadowed anything positive. He cursed his mother for her lack of strength and later his wife in the same way. He cursed his country's weaknesses when he was in the service for their lack of resolve. Between that and their overextended commitments, the loss of a soldier's life was shown to be expendable. Frank also cursed the government for its taxation laws.

"I wouldn't mind but they blow it on frivolous things that don't benefit the people paying." Like many others of his generation who sacrificed their lives, he felt it impossible to ever get ahead. Now in his twilight years he questioned what it was all for.

He cursed the insurance community for its blatant emphasis on profit over human life, disregarding patients like his wife when she was ill. Spiteful he had grown having to care for his wife at a time when they should have been planning for his retirement. Resentful he had become feeling her weakness dragging him down with her each year her sickness carried on.

Had he not suffered enough as a kid? As a soldier? It was something he admitted to often thinking about as he watched the woman he loved wither away. When that shell of a person ceased to be his wife, he welcomed her death.

Yet as deep as the resentment was, he was inconsolable after her passing and greatly mourned her. This was something those at the bar often talked about. No one that I knew of was aware of the source of his bitterness. They just knew him as the local alcoholic. All seemed clueless about the shame he felt for his feelings all the years she was alive battling her sickness.

In the short time I knew the old man, it was clear this guilt and the anger of the past not only ate away at him but ultimately ruined him, transforming him into a weak, feeble elderly man. I think he knew it, too.

Around the Christmas holiday, I asked Frank if he ever prayed, especially when his wife was sick.

Frank found the ritual foolish and snorted at the nonsense. To him, religion was nothing but a waste of time.

Holidays. Church. He knew what they were. Why they existed. Hell, he, and Meredith married in a church at her grandfather's insistence. But that was about the extent Church ever played in his life. "Besides, this grand organization was always too good for its people, praying in Latin when nobody knew what they are talking about and forcing people to donate out of already empty pockets."

"But all that has changed," I told him.

Frank's opinion could not be swayed. He did not want to consider that what I was saying about faith and never being alone held any sort of truth or meaning. That is, until about a week ago.

Though long since dead and buried, Frank's wife was the last of what family Frank had nearby. His brothers were gone and never remained in touch. Gone, too, were his own children. Frank was longtime feeling alone. He was at the bar more often. More troubling was that he was coming in already cocked. Holidays are already rough on vets and older people, but I knew left alone to ruminate on the past nothing in those memories were pleasant. So it was an easy guess that he was drinking most of his days away while at home and not doing much else.

That's why I suggested we check out the lake. But earlier in the McDonald's bathroom I caught him looking in the mirror. It was as if he hardly recognized the gaunt and unshaven face staring back at him.

I wondered if he ever truly opened his heart to those around him. If he was even capable. Or did he just work, fixated on one thing he could easily blame without having to confront feelings he tried so hard to ignore. Or bury.

Putting his recollections in perspective, it was always bitterness of lost opportunities, his job, and his attempts to get ahead that seemed to rule him.

Blowing warm breath into my cold hands, I watched Frank discard his cigarette. He gave it a toss as we made our way back to his truck when we heard a shout. Opening the creaky door to the truck he paused. A half-smile played about his lips. I imagined he was remembering what it was like to be a kid. It was good to see him smile.

"Laura? Mason?" I heard him say unaware that he was most likely recalling his own two children playing beyond the ruins of a house that no longer existed. Somewhere within his line of sight, he was probably even seeing his wife, Meredith, coming into view to gather the children.

Yet, it was a watery, deceitful vision, for those children we heard were not his own.

Cold winter air blew about our faces and I quickly hopped into the vehicle. It was only after he shut his door and rolled down his window that we heard the screams.

Removing himself once more from the Ford, Frank said he was certain the screams were coming from the direction of the pond.

He didn't wait for me. Still familiar with every tree and depression in the ground, he made his way towards the shrieks. It was as if the aging years melted away. Jumping over burnt cinders and crumbled concrete he zigzagged through some of the thick brush that had repossessed what used to be his back yard.

But Frank's view changed when his foot wedged between a split tree that had fallen. He took a hard, painful dive onto the frigid ground. Frozen dirt scraped his knees and leafless branches whipped small cuts into his forehead.

I caught up to him just then and helped him up. "What can I do?" I asked.

The cries were louder now, as was Frank's breathing. "Call 911," he said before taking off again. Heaving his heavy and inflexible frame forward as fast as he could, he made his way to the pond and the children.

Not far behind I was fumbling for my Nokia buried in my jeans front pocket. The child in the purple coat was looking up at Frank as he tried desperately to keep himself out of the cold water.

"Help! My brother!" he cried.

The other child splashed furiously. Both were trapped in a small opening of the ice-covered pond.

While I was pulling the phone from my pocket, Old Man Maguire was stumbling along the water's edge attempting to break a branch off a tree to hand to the kids. But they were too far out. Nothing he was able to get to was long enough.

Testing the ice, Frank dropped to his hands and knees.

"Frank," I yelled. "What are you doing? You'll get yourself killed."

Ignoring me, he inched his way to the drowning boys. But even I could hear the ice under him making scary sounds. Groaning under his weight.

The boys' parents must have also heard the screams. Only after Frank reached the boys, carefully crawling along the ice, did they, too, make it to the pond.

As they neared, Mom crying for her babies, they saw the phone in my hands. But there was nothing I could do. "There's no signal," I told the dad.

Wearing a heavily saturated green and black crocheted hat, the littlest boy's face was an alarming shade of blue. He spoke with quivering lips when Frank grabbed his wrist to keep him from submerging again. "I w-want m-my mommy."

Old Man Maguire was the epitome of cool. He smiled and spoke reassuringly. "Don't worry, son, you're going to be okay."

While struggling to lift the boy, I watched Frank's Marlboros and prized lighter slip free from their pocket behind the overalls. Into the murky water they plopped never to be seen again.

I looked down at my cell phone determined to get a signal. To do something.

"I've got you," I heard Frank say just as I got a signal.

But I turned away to talk to the operator on the other end and noticed the more I walked back towards the truck, the clearer the signal became.

It was then that the ice gave way to Frank's weight. The two went down but the boy's head never again touched the water as Frank hoisted the boy onto the stronger part of the ice nearest the embankment. Then submerging as far as he could go, Frank frantically felt around for the other boy, the boy in purple who lost his grip and nearly succumbed to a watery grave. Braving the stinging cold water, Frank came up for air, held his breath, then went down again.

I get upset retelling the story because if I had only stayed behind maybe I could have done something. Maybe I would have noticed something the parents missed. All I know is that the old man, under frozen water and weighed down by his wet clothes somehow found the other boy, a lifeless form, suspended in the frigid murky water.

From what the dad of the boys later described, Frank lifted the waterlogged boy into the air and onto the ice where the boy's sobbing mother awaited her baby. As the boy touched the ice, his mother wrapped her coat around his helpless little body, cradling him in her arms.

* * *

Even with being in such a rural setting, the ambulance came in time to resuscitate the boy and limit the exposure to hypothermia. With a minor touch of frostbite, the boys were going to be okay thanks to Frank. The parents of the two boys could not believe that the elder sixty-something stranger they waved to earlier was the same man who sacrificed his own life saving the two toddlers.

Though I will never know what Frank saw as his life left him, the dad of the kids said after lifting the second child onto the ice Frank opened his arms and drifted back under the surface without a struggle.

Standing on the edge of the pond, I hoped that all the pain Frank held from so many years of unhappiness, guilt, and hardship, was lifted from him. Watching the boys carried off in layers of blankets and seeing the paramedics and EMTs scattered like ants running through the woods, I was still left awestruck at how calm, cool, and collected Old Man Maguire was. *Serene*, even. Like the universe planned for him to be there. He was at the right place at the right time. It was as if his life was in preparation for this moment.

I cleared my throat as I felt the sting of tears. His kids would have been proud of their father. Even after all he lost trying to live, it would seem he brought purpose and meaning to his life in this one final selfless act. But hadn't he done that when he helped on the farm as a child? Or fought for his country? Or when he became a father? Or when he took care of his wife? At what point does a person recognize and acknowledge they do the best they can with what they have? I thought about how I might... if I might.

Soon the boys who fell in the lake were gone and so were their parents. A different group of emergency workers now stood near the broken ice. Before I witnessed Frank's blue, bloated, lifeless body pulled from the water I, too, was gone. It would have been too painful to watch. It wasn't how I wanted to remember him.

I missed a week of classes to set up the funeral and attend to his affairs, which included cleaning out his place. I don't know if the phone numbers I found were correct but none of his family returned my calls. Cleaning out his apartment for the landlord, I donated Frank's clothes and furniture. From his personal effects, I kept a photo of him from what appeared to be a fishing trip. Shirtless in an NRA cap, he was on a boat. The location of the photo, I didn't realize until much later, was the other side of the lake. Cigarette between his lips, in one hand he held the neck of a nearly empty beer bottle. In the other, a large bass. In the short time I knew him, I had never seen him as happy as he appeared in that photo.

There was no funeral, just a short service a few weeks later when no one came to claim the body. I was the only one in attendance, though my co-workers asked about him.

Just prior, the landlord came to see me at the restaurant. Frank had been his accountant some years back before things got bad. Before Frank was forced to retire. The landlord let him stay at one of his apartments. Never even upped his rent in the nearly fifteen years Frank was there.

"Have a minute?" he asked.

It was a very busy night, but I was able to sneak away for a moment. Outside he gave me an envelope of money.

"What's this?"

"It's his first and last."

That was a lie. I knew the good will this landlord already extended to Frank over the years. Chances were Frank never paid a first and last month's rent. But I could also tell the landlord was a bit emotional about it.

He put a hand over mine. "Take it. Use it towards expenses. Use it towards his burial. I know you've been doing a lot. And I appreciate what you've done, cleaning out the apartment and stuff."

I nodded before I shared a thought. "I think I will get him cremated and scatter the ashes over at the lake."

The landlord smiled. "Yeah, he really loved that place. Can see why he took a shine to you."

I thanked him but indicated that I had to get back to work.

"Here... um, I found this between the floorboards in the bedroom."

I accepted the small box the landlord handed me. "What is it?"

"Something that I think he'd like for you to have."

In the box was a purple heart. From the Korean War.

"I didn't know," I said.

"Not sure anyone else did either."

Holding the medal in my hand, I tried to make sense of the last seven months or so. "So much left unsaid."

"Between you two?"

"No, between him and his family. I mean, I don't talk much with my own family, but..."

The landlord nodded. "Me, neither."

"Not even sure how."

"Same here."

"I so often feel like it's because they're disappointed in me in some way. Like I don't live up to their expectations. And that's why they are always on my case about stuff."

"You the oldest?"

"Yeah," I replied.

"My eldest son echoed the same some years back. Course he was in his 30s when he shared that. He was probably right, too. Check that. He was."

I started to say something but held back. He caught me hesitating and called me on it.

"Go on. Spit it out."

I shook my head. Embarrassed now. "I really gotta get back to work."

He didn't push. "Suit yourself. I understand."

"What's the point?" I asked as he turned to leave. "What's the point of working so hard to get somewhere? How is that a life worth living when it is lost living that way? That's not living."

"Guess some would call that sacrifice," the landlord returned. Upon seeing my dissatisfied reaction, he attempted to explain. "The secret, as I see it, is finding balance. You're young yet. Got the whole world ahead of you. We're always in a rush to get somewhere. To grow up. First, it's 16, right? You wanna drive. Then 18. Hey, you're legal. We're all adults now. Twenty-one. Wow! Now you can drink. Then what? Suddenly we're out there on our own trying to figure out what the hell to do."

He stepped closer. "Work hard to become something of yourself but cherish the things that are important to you. Celebrate the accomplishments. The milestones. You saw something in Frank just as he saw something in you. Use that. Don't take things for granted. Be grateful for every day. The trick is not to lose your identity worried about everyone else around you. Success and happiness... these are things that don't have to be defined by big houses or large bank accounts. It's about learning to make the most of life's moments."

Clearing his throat, he looked away for a moment to run a hand over his face. He then sniffed hard before speaking. "I'm damn near sounding like a Hallmark card, kid. I don't even talk this way to my own."

"No time?" I asked.

"There's always time. Just too embarrassed. Honestly, it's only after I get some beers in me am I able to be on the level with my boy. But even then, I wonder how *he* judges *me*. Imagine that? You're worried about your pop and chances are he's feeling the same way."

I didn't know what to say.

"There's no reason why men have to be ashamed for their feelings," he said.

"My girlfriend's grandfather is like that. The family doesn't really interact with him. I've been told he doesn't talk much."

"But I gather he does with you."

I laughed. "He won't shut up! It's the coolest thing. And we talk about everything!"

"See. Start the dialogue. Others will follow your lead. Everyone is itching to talk. To share. It's just easier to remain on a superficial level. That anger and bitterness Frank felt, I would bet, largely came from not engaging. Holding back. Not admitting to being scared."

"Or alone."

"Or even grateful," he added.

As we parted, the landlord turned back to me one last time on the way to his car. "I think, if anything, Frank's now at peace. Scattering his ashes there at the lake... well, it will mean he's finally home."

Returning to the chaos that was another busy night at the restaurant, my eyes were immediately drawn to his usual spot at the bar. "I hope so," I said aloud thinking of the landlord's words. "I hope so."

GOLDIE

Already devastated by the breakup of his longtime girlfriend, Tristan was inconsolable at the passing of his two aging Italian Greyhound rescues.

"Hey," his friend and teaching colleague of over ten years implored, "you need to get out." Because this wasn't just about the dogs, he took a more direct approach. "Wallowing in pity and depression is doing you no favors."

Tristan shrugged off the concern. "I'm fine," he whispered as he swallowed the rest of his beer. He grimaced at the taste of the lukewarm backwash left in the bottle. Bottled beer never remained cold for long under an August sun.

Noticing one of the dog beds still on the porch, Marty wasn't so sure. An hour earlier, when he used the bathroom, he saw framed photos of Tristan and Debra-Lynn still up on the wall. "Wish I believed that."

"Really," Tristan said. "I'm fine."

Marty shook his head. Tristan had that far-off look in his eyes. "Could have fooled me."

"Just a lot to be hit with at once. Difficult to concentrate on anything else these days."

Marty tried to change the subject. "How's your summer going?"

Tristan snorted. "Not bad, save for watching the little fur babies deteriorate before my very eyes."

Marty carefully navigated Tristan's reply. "Did you work the summer school program in July?"

"Not this year. I did take part in that district workshop that ran for two weeks in June after school got out."

"That's right. You mentioned you might do that. And?"

"And what? It got me out of bed and out of the house. Was surprised I didn't see you there."

Marty was pleased Tristan was starting to come around and engage a bit more in the conversation. "I almost did. Too much union work, though. That and we took the kids to the Cape. Anyway, it's going to be a busy year with contract negotiations and all. You joining us again?"

Tristan shrugged. Then smirked after thinking about it. Being a part of the last two rounds in earlier years, there was no way he'd miss it. "Most likely."

"All right. Good to know." Marty sat back and took in the warm breeze that blew in from his left. He watched it lift the first ply of the folded napkins. The breeze also gently nudged the unattended paper plates closer to the edge of the small table. He moved them closer to the center and placed an empty beer bottle on each of the plates. "Ready for the new school year?"

"Not really. Not yet, anyway. After what happened in April and now the death of the dogs..." Tristan trailed off before speaking again. "Timing couldn't be worse. It's only been a week. I'm sure I will be."

"Yeah," Marty said as he exhaled. "And we report back in two weeks. Kids are back in three. Can't believe Labor Day is almost upon us."

"Well..."

Marty brought his left leg over his right knee as he leaned back in his chair. "Well, what? What're you not telling me?"

"I may not be..." Tristan started, suddenly realizing this was perhaps the first time he was about to say the words aloud.

"May not be what?"

Tristan stifled back a chuckle. He was nervous. Even in front of his friend he didn't know exactly how to express what he was feeling.

"Tristan?" Marty dropped his leg so both feet were on the porch. He leaned forward.

Tristan was being coy. He took his time to answer, focusing instead on removing the label from the brown bottle. "Okay. Here's the skinny." Tristan shifted in his seat before planting his palms on his knees with a slap. "I may not... I'm thinking of not coming back."

"To the same school or our district?" was Marty's immediate response.

"All of it."

"I'm not following."

"I'm done. I want out. I quit."

"Wait. What?"

Tristan shrugged his shoulders and rose from his seat. He pointed at his friend's empty bottle. "Want another before I throw some food on the grill?"

"Nah, I'm good," Marty answered even though his creased brow showed otherwise. "On second thought, have any whiskey?"

| 2 |

"Well, it's not like there's much to count on if she uses my family as an example." Tristan ran his hand over Charlie, an aged male Iggy happily curled in his lap. "What's that saying? 'The apple doesn't fall far from the tree'?"

It was April. Spring break from school. Four months before Tristan dropped his bombshell news. Marty was over checking in on Tristan after receiving a text that Tristan's fiancée and girlfriend of three years had abruptly broken up with him and moved back home to Colorado.

"I think the phrase you're looking for has more to do with how parents are a reflection — a warning — for how their children turn out. Anyway, that's just not right." Marty wasn't sure if he was responding to the woman's sudden move or Tristan's self-loathing.

"That's it exactly. Hey, guys are just as bad, right? Worse, even. We throw around all that stuff about what if the girl we date or *marry* ends up like her mom. Right? We're always observing the moms."

Marty bobbed his head in agreement, fearing exactly what followed.

"For example, how's your mother-in-law?"

"We're not even going there."

Tristan laughed. But Marty had done well for himself. A twenty-year educator, he was a third-grade teacher and president of the teacher's union. Married for ten years, he was also father to two children.

"Face it, Marty," Tristan said with a wink and click of his tongue, "you lucked out. You have a beautiful family."

Marty frowned, displaying visible discomfort with the compliment.

"But it wasn't just that. I know she was tiring of dealing with these little guys." Tristan gestured to the dogs.

"So, then, it wasn't entirely unexpected?"

"I don't know."

"Well, regarding the dogs, I get it. They're like your kids."

"Exactly. I can't tell you how many people who have kids have told me that they appreciated having dogs ahead of time because it was like a warmup before having children of their own."

"Okay," Marty replied somewhat indifferently. Though he himself was a father he had never been a dog owner.

"I know. I know. It's not *exactly* the same. I've been teaching for twenty years, though. I'm not *that* disconnected. I just think too many people dismiss the level of responsibility they need to take on when they take in a pet, especially a rescue. Furthermore, things change when they get old or are adopted already aged. Sick. Infirmed."

"You have a point there."

"These two were in bad shape when I picked them up. They'd been through a lot. While in some ways they seemed to fit right in, there were other things you could tell that still affected them even years later."

To his left on the corner cushion of the sectional was his other Iggy, Winnie. She was tightly curled in her oversized bed. Winnie was a fawn-colored female. Seven years earlier they had come into Tristan's life battered and abused. They were hurting from physical and emotional neglect. As an adult bonded pair, they never left each other's side. It didn't take long before they never left Tristan's side either.

Tristan swore they communicated unlike any other pet he ever had. It was as if they read his mind. Over the years, they had all grown very attached.

"Speaking of shape. How's the female doing?" Marty asked.

"Better. But this is our *new* normal. Whereas Charlie, here, is suffering from blindness and deafness, Winnie's vestibular syndrome episodes really changed her. There are moments she's more aware and her personality shines as bright as it ever did. But she doesn't walk much and needs me to carry her up and down the stairs."

"I'm sorry."

"Thanks. It is what it is. Just sad to watch. I mean, I know they're dogs..." Tristan's eyes moistened. "They've just made so much progress over the years. And Debra-Lynn and I..."

Marty looked up from his cell phone. He had been momentarily distracted by a text regarding a teacher in the district. "You and Debra-Lynn what?" He followed up so Tristan wouldn't think he wasn't listening. "Just a fire I have to put out regarding the principal in the Baker Elementary building."

"No worries. I was just going to say that taking care of them kind of became our thing."

"Yeah, but not everyone is into dogs as much as you."

"This is true." That was a problem he discovered when dating. Even before Debra-Lynn. "There were other things, too. She wanted real kids, Marty, not canine substitutes. I can't begrudge her for that. But she went back to school to pursue a law degree and I just wanted these two seniors to live out their lives however long before caring for a brood of my own."

Marty was amused by his friend's word choice. "Brood?"

"Yeah, brood," Tristan replied with a smile. "Anyway, I guess everything was just taking too long."

"Well, it's not easy juggling all the things that life throws at us," Marty reflected.

"Never thought it was. Hence, my—"

"Dismissal of the idea?"

"No, my apprehension."

"Right."

"I was the same way with buying a house. Took me until I was thirty-four before I took the plunge."

"What took you so long?"

"I was scared."

"Of?"

"Too big a purchase. All that money. A thirty-year mortgage. Thirty years!"

"It is daunting."

Charlie squirmed in Tristan's lap. He tightened his curl to fight off a chill. With so little body fat the breed was notorious for always being cold. Since it was April, it would be a few more weeks before temperatures were consistently warmer in Connecticut. Even the house was cool. Tristan made a mental note to excuse himself shortly to put the dog sweaters in the dryer. He had started a load of wash earlier before Marty arrived.

Marty's cell phone vibrated, alerting him to another text.

"Same situation?"

"Nope. Gotta hit the road. This one is from my wife. Wants me to pick up something from the store on the way home."

"Ah," Tristan acknowledged.

"So, where'd she go, anyway?"

"Debra-Lynn? Back to Colorado."

"Finishing her degree out there, then?"

"I think so. I'm not really sure. I'm not even sure she was attending this semester."

"You did indicate that she was something of a free spirit, right? Restless. Impatient. But driven."

"Very much so. Intelligent, too. Loved talking with her, especially in those earlier days."

"How about the restless part?"

"I think that's why she returned to school in her thirties to get her law degree. She was driven about being something more. Doing more. Having more. In the end, I think that's what led to her restlessness. But I think she's been like that her whole life."

"Makes you wonder if she'll ever find what she's looking for."

"I've been thinking the same. It obviously wasn't me."

"You doing okay, though? Need anything?"

"I have these two," Tristan said, motioning to his Italian Greyhound rescues. "I'm good."

"Right."

Though he couldn't tell if Marty believed him or not, the dogs were a big help. As crushed as he was, things never seemed too bad so long as he had his fur babies. "You know, I was probably holding her back over here anyway. Knowing her, she'll most likely end up becoming an attorney general or something. Maybe even president."

Marty laughed rising from the sofa to take his leave. "Wouldn't that be something?"

| 3 |

"Tristan, the dogs passed away, what, less than four weeks ago. Are you sure about this?"

The friends were sitting in shorts and summer tees under a rising sun set against a clear blue sky outside of a local diner. It was early morning. Though they often met for a late breakfast or early brunch before taking in a science fiction film on the weekend, this was not one of those times. Tristan called Marty to share with him his plans.

With red eyes Tristan attempted to articulate the many emotions running through him at that particular moment. He inhaled deeply. "I don't know. In a way I think it's been a long time coming."

When Tristan first entertained the idea earlier this month, Marty humored him thinking it was grief talking. Yet here he was, just as school was about to begin, talking about leaving again.

Marty placed his fork back onto the plate without even tasting his eggs. His appetite suddenly lost. "How do you mean?"

"Take this past June, the end of the school year. Instead of feeling exhilarated that I had earned another year under my belt I was just so damn exhausted. All over, too. Physically. Mentally. Emotionally. Spiritually."

"Well, Debra-Lynn..."

"No, I get that."

"I knew you seemed way too composed when I visited you in April. And this summer's declining health of the dogs. Not that they were getting any younger." Marty used the fingers from his right hand to emphasize the multiple things Tristan had been through. "Then there's the fallout from the divorce your parents went through a couple of years back. Your estranged dad. The passing of some of your oldest friends of the family over the last three, four years. You've had a challenging year. Several challenging years! Much of it at the same time Debra-Lynn was in your life."

"This was different, though. I mean, up until April I was looking at the last few years feeling pleased that I made it through those years of teaching unscathed."

"Or so you thought. But are you sure it's not just a perfect storm of events?"

"Honestly, people would probably just call the last few years... life. Right? We all have crap that happens that we must deal with on a regular basis. But in June, once I was home and things settled, I was suddenly struck with just how lucky I was to have *made* it through another year on the front lines. I was looking at it as if I had *survived* something. What's with that? That's not how we should be reflecting on our time in the classroom. In the profession."

"I don't know. It's understandable. Been tough all around, really. From a union standpoint you know how difficult things have been for the profession. It's everywhere, too. Discipline problems in the schools. No accountability. Teachers pushing boundaries with students or failing to be professional with their colleagues. Administrators overstepping their authority. So many fires that need putting out before they become full-blown scandals. Then there's the ongoing budget battles. Budget cuts. That's why we've been protesting these last few years at the state capitol. It's why we are always meeting with HR. In another week we have our first contract negotiation meeting. It's that time already. Every year things seem to get harder. That's a lot of pressure whether you are a union member or officer, teacher, or classroom aide. And let's be mindful of the pressure the administrators are under as well."

"It would be nice if we at least had the support of the community," Tristan remarked knowing full well he was preaching to the choir. A part of him felt as if articulating these points aloud would finally validate them. "Speaking of admins, I don't know about you, but it's getting harder and harder to work with those who continue to take the word of a student or a parent over ours. It's as if they could care less about parameters we set in our class. Can't send them to the office because they get sent back and suddenly *we're* the bad guys. Here we are trying to prepare young people for a future outside of the school bubble and all we're creating are victims — snowflakes — who will be unaccountable and irresponsible members of the community."

"So many variables there, though," Marty defended. "Among them, too many instances where the rules apply to some but not all. But that requires an administrator, or superintendent really, with a backbone to stand up to the board or parents. It requires leaders who are ready to empower and support their staff, not cower under pressure because it's too difficult to stand up for what is right, for what they'd want someone in their position to do if they were back in the classroom. So, what we end up with is inconsistency."

"That's just it. How many administrators haven't even cut their teeth in the classroom, yet they're going to tell you — no, *dictate* to you — what you should be doing."

"Well, that's why districts love bringing them in. The board and the powers that be downtown get to mold these individuals to toe the party line, as it were."

"And don't even get me started on evaluations. I have to laugh when I hear of this one administrator, formerly a gym teacher, coming around to evaluate core subject teachers. Really?"

Marty raised his eyebrows as Tristan paused to take a sip of his coffee.

"My favorite," Tristan continued, "are those teachers who fake a fine *performance* at the time of evaluation. The rest of the time? The kids don't get any homework. There are no due dates for anything. No real discipline. No real accountable adherence to the pacing guide or curriculum."

"You sound jealous," Marty toyed.

Tristan sniggered. "Well, they are the ones who make us teachers who care, putting in the time to challenge the kids, look bad."

Marty shooed a fly from trying to land on his plate. Then he leaned back and crossed his legs before speaking again. "The same can be argued for directly associating student scores with evaluations."

"Especially if the classroom is a war zone. I'm not saying that those who disrupt a class are always acting out maliciously. It's quite the opposite. I know it's often because of their own frustrations, things they are dealing with in school and at home. I get that. But if we continue to reward those with poor behavior in a mainstream class and fail to recognize those who aspire to achieve, be it academically or whatever, because some feel it would be *unfair* or it might make the few disrupters *feel* bad, we're, in effect, telling — no, we're showing — those who work hard and follow the rules that it isn't worth it. That the only way you're going to get recognized is if you, too, become a disrupter. I mean how many times are we supposed to continue rewarding kids for doing what is expected of everyone else in the school? What the hell is that going to look like when we start doing the same thing in the real world? You know, granting leniency to some who commit crimes or loot or cause damage to private and public property? Will everyone else have to still obey the law at that point? Will anyone even feel safe?"

"I think that's a little different."

"Is it? How many teachers feel safe or supported in their classrooms with the way some of these kids are acting these days? How many teachers feel they can speak up without reprisals? They don't even fill out the anonymous surveys the union sends because they fear the board or downtown will be able to identify them by their IP address."

Tristan was venting. Unintentionally letting loose. But Marty knew otherwise. "What is it, really, Tristan? What's going on?"

Tristan looked to his friend. "I think it's obvious. I've been teaching for nearly thirty years. It's getting more and more difficult to let things slide or remain silent. To watch those who do what they're supposed to lose out on a good education. To watch those who need specialized attention be addressed with a band-aid approach. In the last few weeks, I think I've come to the conclusion that I just can't do this anymore."

"So, you're going to retire?"

"If only! I can't retire. I mean I have a sizable chunk of savings, but I was thinking more along the lines of... moving."

"Moving? Where?"

"The Pacific Northwest. Seattle."

"Why would you move out there some three thousand miles away?"

"Don't know. Freedom?"

"Freedom?" Marty asked, a crease forming across his brow. "You sure you don't mean escape?"

"I don't think so, even though that may be the farthest I can go while living in the continental United States."

"Not interested in Hawaii?"

"Don't want to be trapped on an island. Besides, Debra-Lynn's from Colorado—"

Marty made a face. "So this is about Debra-Lynn?"

"No, it's not. Really. It's just that I loved Colorado. Been thinking more along the lines of Wyoming, though. Montana, even. But Seattle, Washington seems to be where it's at for the moment. So much better than Connecticut."

Marty pursed his lips and nodded. "I see."

"Something different. Different atmosphere. Different location. Different people."

Marty couldn't argue there. Businesses had been steadily leaving the state of Connecticut for years. Long considered by outsiders to be a wealthy state, the wealth part was primarily concentrated in only a handful of towns. Maybe a dozen. That's a dozen out of nearly two hundred. And the town they taught in was *the* perfect example of just how bad the housing crisis was in their New England state. Between the foreclosures and short sales, it was a paradise for buyers. Sellers not so much since homes were undervalued.

Marty took a sip of his water. "You don't think you're projecting?"

"Oh, I've no doubt there's a lot going on here. Projection. Evasion. But there's also disillusionment. Guilt. Sometimes we need to go to extremes to—"

"Well, now."

"You know what I mean."

"Do I? This is all very sudden. Debra-Lynn left six months ago. Are you sure you want to uproot in such a drastic and finite way? Wouldn't taking a leave of absence be better? You're going someplace where you have no family. No friends. No job yet."

"Four."

"Huh?"

"Debra-Lynn. Four. She left four months ago, not six," Tristan corrected.

"Okay. Yes. Debra-Lynn left *four* months ago." After a beat, Marty then posed an obvious question. "Do you plan on teaching out there?"

"Don't know. I just know it is time for a change. Hey, at least with the dogs, I felt there was some kind of balance in my life. No matter what happened during the day, I came home to a kind of happiness that I seriously never knew until they came into my life. Sounds weird, I know. But even if I couldn't travel or go very far on account of them, there was always this joy that came from having them in my life."

"That's how people feel about having children, too."

Tristan made a face. "Ouch." It was not lost on Tristan that Marty's comment was like a point Debra-Lynn made before leaving.

Marty shrugged.

"Well," Tristan continued, "right now I can't even walk around my backyard without breaking down. The house... the silence is — get this — deafening! How can it be any quieter?

Never mind that the bed is empty. Even without Debra-Lynn, I always had Charlie who would curl up in my arms every night. I leaned my head against him more than I did my own pillow. Now? Now there's no one. There's no Debra-Lynn. No Winnie. No Charlie. No balance. I feel a wreck."

"I hear you. Perhaps you should see someone."

Tristan shook his head, dismissing the idea. "Since I've always been so caught up with the dogs on account of their health... I mean, I can see why Debra-Lynn left. I just thought we were a team when it came to them. But I guess it's just been me all along."

"The dogs were a part of *your* life before Debra-Lynn. It makes perfect sense. You've been caring for them for years. Didn't mean they had to be her responsibility, though."

"I had hoped it was something we'd be able to share. I thought it was something we *were* sharing. But she wanted kids. A family. The dogs didn't do it for her."

"They were how old?"

"Eighteen."

"They both went on the same day?" Marty asked, suddenly realizing he didn't know the specifics behind their passing.

"Charlie passed in my arms. Took the entire morning. Weird thing was he was fine the night before. I had Winnie put down when the vet came to pick up Charlie."

"Oh, wow. I didn't know."

"She'd been declining faster than Charlie. I think she would have been okay if I could have been home all the time for her, like during the summer months. But she was in tough shape. At the time, the thought of returning to school and leaving her all day without companionship... I don't know. Figured it would have been unnecessarily difficult for her. She could barely function these last couple of months as it was."

"But you're still grieving. And that loss is made ever more... it is exacerbated by Debra-Lynn's departure. I'd go so far as to say it's the culmination of the last several years with *all* that's been going on in your life."

"You may be right."

"But you're still resolute in your plans to move?"

"House is already up for sale."

"Since when?"

"Last week."

"Really? I haven't seen a sign out front."

"Not putting one out there. In fact, I'm not telling anyone until the week I do move."

"Why?"

"Indeed. Why? Whose business is it anyway?"

"You don't want anyone to talk you out of it, do you?"

"I'm not sure they could. I really can't stay here anymore. And it's not just this town. It's this state. I need to make a change. A radical change."

"So, what is it, then? Why the secrecy? The subterfuge? The coyness?"

"Two things. One, I don't want to deal with having to explain or defend myself to others, be it friends or family. Not everyone knows what I've been through these last few years. Those that do, unlike you, only know bits and pieces."

"And the second?"

"Well..." Tristan began, his voice dropping to a whisper. "What if I fail in my attempt to get out of Dodge?"

For the first time that morning, Marty understood. In a strange way, he even envied Tristan.

"Okay," Marty said, motioning to the server for the check. She just wrapped with another customer two tables down and he was trying to catch her before she went back inside. "I hope you find whatever it is you are looking for. Whatever you need, I'm here. Just let me know."

| 4 |

"Think you'll ever get another dog?"

"If I stayed," Tristan replied over the phone, "Maybe. It's been crippling without the two of them around. But more so with the driving. You'd think I had companion dogs or something, not pets. Leading up to the move, well, let's just say it's a good thing I was busy juggling so much. Good distraction."

"You're missing all the fun over here while you're out there on the road," Marty then said.

"At school? Or are you referring to contract negotiations?"

"Both. We have a new principal at one of the buildings."

"Yeah? And?"

"Not good. Not good at all. Not sure why they moved her up when they had a strong candidate who is already in the building. The staff is, at this stage, ready to walk out. I'll be surprised if she makes it to Christmas."

"Oh, wow," Tristan emphatically replied. "It's *that* bad?"

"It's *that* bad."

"How are contract negotiations going?"

"Thought we'd be farther along."

"How's the board's attorney this year? Same guy or a new one? That other one they had a few years ago was something else. I don't know that I've ever used the word bloviate before. He, though, was a bloviator. Like to the point where his picture should be next to the word in a dictionary."

"Yeah, that was fun."

"And how are things in the district, aside from the school you mentioned?"

"The usual. You know. Administrators who overstep their authority. Teachers who don't think clearly and blur the lines of professionalism."

"You were right, then."

"About?"

"The fun," Tristan answered with a laugh. "Lots and lots of fun stuff."

"Yeah." Marty chuckled before changing the subject. "Drove by your house today on the way home."

"It's still standing, I hope."

"It is. And I saw some cars in the driveway."

"Probably the realtor, Mario. Yeah, he worked some fine magic finding a buyer so quickly."

"So, you're out. Free and clear?"

"Not really. Still need to wait for the buyer's paperwork to go through."

"When do you think that will be?"

"Could be any time now. With Thanksgiving a little over a week away, it might not be until December."

"That's kind of what we're looking at for contract negotiations. Will probably wrap up sometime in mid-December."

"It was probably impulsive to take off as early as I did, leaving the house vacant. Could have probably held out longer to get more for the house, too. I just needed some distance. Didn't see the need to hang around since I wasn't teaching. Would have been so much more difficult. Plus, I don't know what weather

I am going to encounter at the higher elevations the deeper we get into fall."

"Where are you now?"

"Jersey."

"Jersey? You're practically still next door."

"I know. I know. Haven't gotten very far. Yet."

"When are you planning to reach the west coast?"

"Thanksgiving is probably the safest bet. I'll play it by ear. Wanna be able to take my time. Given the weather, though, I should probably try to stick to that timetable."

"Yeah, they're calling for snow over here later in the week."

"I saw that. By the way, you're never going to believe what happened to me."

| 5 |

Tristan approached the service counter at the back of the dealership after hanging up with Marty. Day two into his trek westward and he was already having truck problems.

"So, what's the damage?" After settling the bill, he was hoping to get back on the road in time to reach the Best Western in Scranton where he had reservations.

The young woman behind the counter shut him down, however, holding up her index finger as she answered the phone. Even this late in the day, Tristan was surprised by how much the phone was ringing. The dealership was big. More than that, it had a massive service shop. Both the showroom and service area were consistently busy for the entire day.

But finding himself in a dealership getting work done on his truck only a day into his trip was probably fortuitous. He didn't want to hypothesize dealing with a similar situation in the middle of nowhere, say a solitary highway in Nebraska, where there are only fields for miles and no cell service.

Earlier he half-joked with Marty how this better not be a sign of things to come. As rash as a sudden trip across country seemed, he was meticulous about addressing every detail — or as many he was in control of — ahead of the move, from selling the house to moving his belongings ahead of time to having his black Ford 150 serviced and prepped for cross-country travel. And yet, here he was. In New Jersey. At a Ford dealership. At 5:30 in the evening. Still, with most of his belongings already on their way to Seattle, the red engine light couldn't have picked a better time to come on considering he was only a day into his trip and still very much around civilization. And cell phone towers.

Tristan leaned against the service desk, resting an elbow on the counter. Off to his right, he noticed a short-statured couple in the waiting room area. They looked bored. Exhausted.

He could empathize. It was a long day for him, too. Still had a two-to-three-hour drive ahead of him before he could call it a night. At least the mechanics were able to accommodate him and address his engine pistons problem the same day he stopped in. Had that not been the case, he would have been delayed at least a day. Maybe two.

He again reflected on his situation. Just twenty-four hours in and this is how the trip was unfolding. Tristan couldn't help but wonder what other *fun* was in store.

Stealing another glance at the short couple, his attention wasn't so much drawn to them as it was to what they were taking turns holding — a black and white Italian Greyhound. If not for the blueish white eyes indicating blindness, the elderly dog in their arms was nearly the spitting image of his recently deceased Charlie.

Tristan grinned broadly at the memory of his own Iggies. Watching the senior dog respond to the showering of love and affection it was getting from the couple pulled at Tristan's heart strings. It was enough to tap into the grief he still felt for their loss.

"Oh, boy," he muttered as he turned to the girl at the service desk who was hanging up the phone. Well aware that his eyes were quickly moistening, he did his best not to let it show.

"What's wrong?" she asked.

Tristan looked at the young lady wistfully before blurting out a confession. "I think I just realized something. I don't know that I'll ever be able to adopt another dog. There'll be no coming back from losing another."

| 6 |

Day eight into the drive west, Tristan was entering Cheyenne, Wyoming. At six thousand feet above sea level, the air here was different than he was used to in New England. Back east, his town in Connecticut was only three hundred feet above sea level.

According to the radio station, an evening weather event was imminent prompting an upcoming closure of the Interstate 80 highway in both directions. Luckily, there were only flurries to contend with throughout most of the day's drive. Though cozy in the truck, it was very windy at this elevation. And very cold.

Coming off the highway, Tristan turned left off the exit ramp. He was aiming to settle for the night at a place he saw advertised on a billboard when a furball of a dog darted across the road in front of both him and an oncoming car in the other lane.

Oblivious to the dog, the car barely missed clipping it. Even though Tristan had enough time to see the situation unfold, he still had to slam on the brakes. The truck came to a stop slightly angled to the left and just over the center yellow line after failing to find traction on the slippery road. Tristan cursed himself for not having the four-wheel drive engaged. This secondary road was surprisingly worse than the highway even though it didn't seem to have much snow sticking to it. Given the weather conditions, the temperature, and the declining sunlight as afternoon gave way to early evening, it would have been the smartest and safest thing he could have done once he took the exit. He needed to remind himself he was no longer on the east coast.

Taking a deep breath to calm himself, Tristan then maneuvered the truck off the road and joined up with the older man he noticed trailing after the dog.

| **7** |

"What kind of dog are ya looking for?" the old man asked.

"No. Not looking for any dogs." Tristan smiled as he shook his head. "My fiancé and I used to care for two rescued Italian Greyhounds, though."

"Dem aren't the big jobs, are they? Run like bobcats?"

Tristan laughed. "The Italian Greyhounds are a small breed. But yeah, they sure do run fast. Some twenty-five, thirty miles an hour."

"So they race, no?"

Tristan shook his head. "Not that I am aware of. Maybe in some countries."

"Huh."

"But they are a majestic breed. The embodiment of love wrapped in tiny statuesque bodies." Tristan then checked himself. Thinking about his babies made him feel all warm and fuzzy. He wasn't sure if the gentleman sitting across from him was the warm and fuzzy type.

"Got me a guy who does some work for me around the place. Had to give up their girl so I'm fosterin' her while lookin' for a good home."

Tristan did a double take. "Oh, so she's not yours?"

Just a short time earlier Tristan helped the old man — whose full name was Barnaby but went by Barnes — locate the dog in a field parallel to the road. Barnes then invited Tristan to his home to warm up. But not before Tristan pulled his truck off the road and onto Barnaby's property. He did this while Barnes leashed the dog and walked her back to his place.

"No. But she could be. *Yours*, that is."

Tristan was taken aback. "Oh, I don't know."

"Course I understand she's not one of those running rat critters you're used to having."

"What breed is she exactly?" Tristan asked. When he first saw her run across the road, given the dog's thick brown and black coat, he was sure it was a young German Shepherd.

"Not sure. Vet claims it's a Shepherd mix. Most likely a Golden Shepherd on account that it looks to have some Retriever in her."

Tristan nodded silently. He had been petting the sitting dog, whose golden-colored hair was luminous in the light of the living room fire. Without warning, she suddenly flatted herself to roll over onto her back. Positioning herself into an arc, it was as if she was trying to form the letter *c* with her body. She then wagged her tail. It made a thudding sound each time it hit the floor.

"You know what that means, don't ya?" the old man asked.

"No, what?"

"It means she trusts you. She's baring her belly. And she's an old bird. Up near ten, eleven years old. Don't trust too easy. Damn mutt don't even trust *me* much."

And yet, here she was on her back. Eyes squinty. Mouth partly open so her front teeth showed. She looked quite comfortable. Tristan was amused by the dog's expression.

Tristan rubbed the dog's chest. Ran his hand to her belly then back up to her chest before petting her around her neck. "Is that why she was out in the road? Trust issues?"

Barnes seemed flustered by the question. "Had the gate to the property fence open for a moment. Split second, I tell ya. Damn thing scooted right past when I wasn't lookin'."

"Lucky she didn't get hit."

"Already was."

Tristan was horrified. "Good God. When? Not today, though, right? Was she okay?"

"Didn't seem to be too bad. It was in late July, early August. She got back up and seemed to brush it off. Girl's hardy, I tell ya. Reckon her lame hip is a souvenir from that strike, though."

"Oh, wow. Poor thing."

"Aww, she's a good girl. Just uptight at times. Stressed. Seems to be searching for something. Dunno. Easily spooked, too. Probably 'cause she's been given up so many times."

"Animals certainly know more and feel more than we give them credit for."

"Got that right," Barnes agreed. "But she's been through at least three or four owners in her lifetime."

"Why?"

"Can't really say. Just that it never seemed to be because of her, from what I was told. Just a matter of circumstance, I s'pose."

"Squatty thing, isn't she? Such short legs. Looks like she has some Corgi blood in her. Can't get over the size of those big paws, though."

"Definitely a mixed breed. Got a coat and the bark of a German Shepherd. Scares the shit out of people now. Damn near gave me a heart attack the first time I heard her. Sheds something fierce, too. Sheds enough hair to cover a dozen of yer rats."

Tristan chuckled. He couldn't imagine a dog shedding *that* much. Then again, all of his prior rescues were senior Iggies. Iggies were short-haired. "How much would you say she weighs?"

"Dunno for certain. 'Bout thirty, thirty-five. Give or take a few."

The old man stood with difficulty to throw another log on the fire. Shadows were long, making it difficult to identify the newspapers, magazines, and other items piled in the crowded room. But it was cozy, nonetheless. The paneled walls and wooden décor were what one out-of-stater would expect to find in Wyoming.

"Well, I should probably go," Tristan said after some silence. He enjoyed talking with the man and spending some time with the dog, but it had grown dark. The flurries were turning into a steadier snowfall. "It's getting late," Tristan said. "And it's already snowing."

Barnes was closely watching Tristan and the dog interact. Tristan had been giving the dog a healthy dose of chest rubbing. During this time, she kept a paw on his arm. Whenever he'd pause, she'd then use her paw to push or pull his hand back to her.

"Sure you won't reconsider?"

Tristan admitted aloud what was becoming clearer the longer he spent with her. "Another breed may be just what I need to help me get over the loss of my Iggies."

"Well, what's stoppin' ya?"

"Not sure. How much you want for her?"

"If you're serious about taking her and giving her a good home, she's yours. Fer free."

Tristan looked up from the dog. "Really?" He had gone from the chair to squatting to kneeling beside the dog. "I'm still on the road, though. Probably won't reach Seattle for a few days yet."

"She'll be fine. Loves going on drives."

Tristan grinned.

"You from around here?"

"No. I'm actually from the east coast."

"Visited Rocky Point out there in Rhode Island back when I was a teenager."

Tristan's eyes went wide. "You're kidding! Rocky Point! Really?"

Though the old man had been friendly and personable, he hadn't smiled much except for a few closed-mouth instances. As he spoke of Rocky Point, however, there was a gleam in his eyes. At Tristan's recognition of the park, he grinned broadly, revealing a few missing teeth.

"Was never much interested in them there Six Flags parks. Hershey's. Disney. But always fondly remembered Rocky Point," Barnes shared.

"Nothing can beat the Shore Dinner Hall, that's why."

Another smile from the old man. Tristan wondered if Barnes met a girl there. Perhaps his wife. If he was married at one time.

"Don't know that I ever ate so much in my life," Barnes recalled.

"Manhattan Clam Chowder and fritters. No one makes them better."

"Nope."

"Even on Cape Cod. There are some good places for chowder. But it's not Manhattan style. And their fritters, while good, are not nearly as good as Rocky Point's."

"Is it still around?"

"No. They tore it down to make room for condos on the water. Guess there was a lot of mismanagement responsible for its downfall. Been about twenty years now, though it was a ghost town, er park, about a decade before that. But the chowder and clam fritters are supposedly still being sold."

"Where the park was?"

"No. I guess there are a few locations throughout Rhode Island. Again, I'm not sure of the specifics. I can attest to having some at a sit-down location some ten years ago though."

"That must have been nice."

"It really was. Just as good as I remembered."

During their reminiscing, the dog opened her eyes and was intensely watching Tristan.

Barnes noticed the dog eyeing the New Englander. "Had my sister's kid put up an ad on that Craig's listing thing. Think he also did something with Bookface too."

"You mean Facebook?"

The old man looked confused. "What'd I say?"

"Bookface."

"It's not Bookface?"

"No, it's actually called Facebook."

"Aw, hell. Anyway, I've had stuff out over the Internets for a couple of months on and off. Can't say I was comfortable with the likes of those who done came around. Neither was she, to be honest. Seems to have taken a shine to you, though. I mean it. Right from the start she's been acting different with you. Affectionately watching yer every move."

"Nice of you to say," Tristan replied, returning his attention to the pretty girl on the floor before him. Flooded by a host of emotions, Tristan was at once excited by the possibilities of having another canine companion and anxious about the unknowns. He had to think about it. Maybe even sleep on it.

Just as Tristan stood, the dog rolled over and stood up as well. While Tristan contemplated his next steps, the dog leaned her head against his right leg. He patted the side of her snout, as if to comfort her. Reassure her. But it was what the dog did after he patted her that truly moved him. She placed her snout in his hand.

"She's never done that there with me," Barnes admitted. "Come to think of it, never seen her do that with anyone."

Tristan swore he heard the old man's voice crack a bit.

"You must be a calming presence for her. You may not have made up your mind, but she sure has."

Tristan squatted before the dog and cupped her muzzle in his hands. He rubbed her ears and ran his fingers around her eyes. She surprised him by leaning forward and giving him two licks, one on the chin and one on the nose.

"You're a good girl, huh," Tristan said. Addressing Barnes, he asked: "Sure I can't give you anything for her?"

"How's about spotting me a couple a bucks fer her feed, if you can spare it. She's current on all shots. Have her paperwork in the other room."

"Sure thing. Be my pleasure."

* * *

Old man Barnes chose to remain inside at the doorway when Tristan left with the dog. Out the door, the dog was at Tristan's heels, trotting proudly like a show dog. Head up. Tail up. Her lead loose every step of the way. She walked alongside him down the snowy drive as if she had been his pet for years, not minutes.

Dropping the tailgate, Tristan expected his belongings to come tumbling out. He breathed a sigh of relief to discover things didn't shift all that much. This made it easier to move around his packed personals to find a place for the dog food.

Coming around to the door behind the driver's seat, Tristan turned to his new companion. "You sure about this?" he asked as he placed her doggy bed on the bench in the extended cab.

She answered the moment he stepped back. Astounding Tristan, the elder pup hopped right into the truck unaided and without command. Lame leg and all. She then planted herself in her bed as she smacked her lips. Like a sentinel, she sat facing forward with purpose. Ready for the journey before her. Tristan wondered if the dog knew something he didn't.

"You're a special one, aren't you?" he whispered as he pulled a blanket from below the bench and bunched it up around her.

"Take care now," Tristan heard Barnes yell from the doorway. "Though I trust you two will take care of each other."

Tristan turned and waved goodbye. "What's her name?" He realized only then that he didn't recall Barnes calling her by name.

"Goldie," came the response.

"Goldie," Tristan repeated. The dog turned to face Tristan upon hearing her name. Her floppy ears popped up and she cocked her head.

Wide, thoughtful eyes stared back at him. She was hanging on his every word.

"Well, *Goldie*, looks like it's just you and me now."

She barked in response.

He ran his hands several times along the length of her muzzle, over her ears, and down her neck before planting a kiss on the side of her big head. There was the whiff of Barnaby's place in her fur. Mostly the aroma of the pine wood burned in his fireplace. But she also had that scent Tristan knew and loved. Embedded deep in her two coats was the toasty warm blanket smell he remembered first picking up on from pets he had in his youth. It was also the smell Tristan would fall asleep to when Charlie was alive. Inseparable, Charlie would often join him at night to curl up in Tristan's arms. Tristan would then fall asleep using Charlie as his pillow.

Goldie brought her wet nose up to his and gave him a lick.

"Yeah," Tristan remarked, "you and me are going to be just fine."

ONE NIGHT IN BANGKOK

H er big brown eyes would not leave the sweaty, dirty man who sat across from me. Even with kids laughing and playing Malaysian wicker volleyball barefoot on the dirt street behind us, there was no distracting her.

It was hot. Unbelievably humid. Because the water was not to be trusted, beer or spirits were the beverages of choice. Man and beast were equally affected.

Even the packs of hounds usually running loose through the streets were taking it easy, their tongues nearly falling out of their wide-open panting jaws.

But not her. Not Dog. Her pointy ears, usually pricked and alert, were flattened back. Lips quivering, her intense and alert gaze said it all.

Dog was not even my pet. Yet she had come to adopt me, nevertheless. Not the other way around.

I first came upon the snarling cur just days before the Siamese coup d'état when I presented a peace offering in the form of some cooked meat. Just a little left over from a street vendor purchase. She, like us all here, was a consequence of her surroundings. Trust did not come easily. It was something to be earned. But from that moment forward, I had a follower.

Life couldn't have been easy for the stray. That much was certain. Though the city was a place one could hide and lay low, it was a rough, violent life here in these parts. And it was about to get worse. Distrust in the monarchy and a growing aversion to outsiders who never seemed to respect the culture or its people made for some perilous exchanges. Especially if you didn't know your way around.

Dog's scarred snout and missing ear flap only hinted at her journey. She was also a mangy lass. But in these two weeks since, she was always within earshot. Sneaking away at times, she would find me shortly thereafter keeping pace whenever I moved about.

She even joined me on the Klongs, sitting like a sentry at one end of the boat while we passed the stilted shacks. Nose high up in the air. I think she appreciated the breeze. And enjoyed the various scents.

Though the markets offered fresh food and the floating restaurants offered tasty fare, the smell everywhere else along the canals wasn't pleasant at all. It was something you got used to. The murky water, cluttered with boats, was used as much for drainage as it was for travel. Recreation. And cleaning clothes.

Full of carp, the waterways were also home to large water dragons. Every time we hit a choppy wave or water splashed onto us, I feared for my companion. Would Dog get sick from the dirty water? Would she become dinner for the dragons?

Answering to the name Dog, my companion — and perhaps my protector — did not trust this eely man sitting across from us. Did not trust his scent. His tone. His shiftiness.

"Well, now," the stranger said backpedaling. "Let's not lose our focus here. No need to jump to hasty conclusions." Just moments ago, his confidence was damn near offensive. So certain was he that he'd be able to swindle me, his smugness was on full display. "We did have a deal now, didn't we?"

All that changed thanks to Dog. I had seen Dog earlier in the day. Like me, she went about her own schedule. Her own routine. It wasn't until I caught her out of the corner of my eye shortly after we sat down that I knew she was back. Throughout the conversation Dog kept moving in. Carefully observing, she'd pace the perimeter a bit before dropping low, keeping her movements subtle so as not to be noticed. Even with the bustling crowds weaving in and around the area her eyes never left us.

But they were a distraction. And I don't know that she liked what she saw. Maybe she knew something about this shady character across from me that I didn't. It appeared the Siamese were right to be wary of foreigners.

At this moment, Dog was off to my left. Though seated on her haunches, she was now fully visible. And audible. Judging by the man's eyes shifting from me to the mongrel, her presence was definitely known. Instead of watching the both of us, she was zeroed in on the stranger. Her growl a rumbling and guttural vocalization. Dog was making the man nervous. I sensed she possessed an innate ability to recognize deception. Never did I trust a mutt more than at this moment.

And yet Dog's protestations, which grew louder, didn't seem to deter the man from slowly withdrawing something large and metallic from his pocket.

Or perhaps it was *because* of the dog that he went for whatever was concealed.

No matter. He thought he was being clever under the cover of dusk. Subtle. Sneaky. But he spoke with a forked tongue. "Let's just first see about ridding ourselves of this bi—"

At once Dog was standing.

There was a throaty bark.

A blur.

Then a horrific scream.

The commotion was brief. The mongrel was soon after resting triumphantly at my feet. Some area onlookers casually glanced from me to the dog to the stranger before going about their usual business. The stranger, clutching his right hand close to his chest, took off running. He left behind a rusted pistol. And a dark pool of red.

Smacking her bloodied lips, Dog ran her tongue over the left side of her snout. Then over the right. Uttering a loud gagging sound, she opened her jaws wide before heaving three digits onto the ground in front of her.

OLD LANGE SYNE

I t would have been easier to go to the grocery store down the street. Instead, Amanda drove to a store two towns over just so she wouldn't bump into any of her students. An easy drive down a winding avenue, she was there in less than thirty minutes. Not bad for a late afternoon on New Year's Eve.

The drive was nice enough this time of year and the roads weren't too slick. She hadn't been out this way in some time and enjoyed the view of the decorated lawns, even though that wasn't her kind of thing.

When the street forked, Amanda stayed to the left as the road fed into another street and then into sprawling suburbia, one that was more affluent than where she currently lived. Here the traffic was also much denser. A sign that the grocery store would most likely be packed. She was in the center of town. Part of her wished she had braved the one closest to home, regardless of who she'd run into. But this way she didn't have to worry about makeup or pleasantries. Quick run in. Quick run out.

Amanda parked away from the entrance to avoid other cars and runaway carriages. She knew better. She chuckled that she was too much like her father who often did the same when she was growing up. Something her mother, if she were still alive, would have chastised her about — especially for parking so far away from the store. Still, the rationale was sound. It was evening. There were crowds. And it was a holiday. People were distracted. Best way to avoid an accident? Anticipate it before it occurs. Ergo, *therefore*, park as far away as you can. Besides, she didn't mind walking.

As it was, just getting to the building was like playing a game of *Frogger* in the parking lot. Still, she kept her wits about her. It was, after all, the holiday season. Smile. Get what's needed and then *no stores* for another week or two she promised herself.

Actually, that wasn't true. If she saw her dad in the next couple of days, she would probably have to pick something up for him. She previously hooked him up with deliveries through Amazon and Stop & Shop's Pea Pod. These eased the burden on them both, even if her father was only about a thirty-minute drive away — much closer than the hour and fifteen commute when both her parents were alive.

The Santa at the door beside the Salvation Army kettle was ringing the bell with way too much holiday spirit. Especially since Christmas ended a week ago. "Merry Christmas!" he repeated enthusiastically.

Amanda nodded at the gentleman as she found herself stuck waiting for the automatic entrance door to open. "I'll get you on the way out." She wasn't even sure the guy in the red suit even heard her. She was only trying to mask the embarrassment she felt for not tossing any coins into the kettle.

The store was decorated beautifully, as stores were this time of the year. That was never the problem. It was her view on holidays, the consumerism of it all — even the entranceway Santa Claus — that was always a turn off.

She recalled as a child her mother giving her and her sister Sears and JCPenny catalogs to write out wish lists. Exciting as this might seem to most children, she never went crazy with it. And even when she picked stuff out, she felt awkward about it. As she grew older, her discomfort with receiving gifts only worsened. She was happier giving than receiving. Not just on holidays, either, but throughout the year. Amanda believed in doing things for people out of good will and kindness not because a holiday dictates that you must.

Watching a woman accompanying her elderly mother made her think of her own. Mom passed away a year before her husband. Ravaged by cancer, the family was sure she had beaten it. As is often the case, it returned. The last six months of it were hell. It had taken its toll on Amanda's father, and it hit home hard for Amanda too.

Amanda's souring of the holidays began when she was a young girl. Happy memories of family holidays or special events were rare. All too often arguments between her mother and father, deaths in the family, or inclement weather would cast a pall over it all. And her mother would be devastated, spending days in a deep depression sobbing.

Amanda then thought of Randy, her high school sweetheart. Randy was the first boy she ever truly loved. Counting high school, they were together for nearly ten years. Though they never married, she always considered him her first husband.

Coming from a big family Randy was all about the holidays. Even when they were still in school. So once again seasonal celebrations took on a greater importance until the end of their relationship when the same things that she watched her mom go through began happening. Sad events that were part of life began to encroach on — and even ruin — the holidays. When they didn't, she would inevitably wait for the shoe to drop.

But that was before she experienced a life-changing event. Before her breakup with Randy. After that things were different. She learned to not only take care of herself but to focus more on gratitude. Daily gratitude.

It's how she was able to process her mother's sickness and death. It was how she was able to return to teaching. It was how she was able to start writing. More importantly, it was how she met Brett. And with Brett, they were all about making every day a holiday. Every day was a celebration of life. Of love. Every day an expression of gratitude. To each other. To the world around them.

"Dee?"

Amanda was in the dairy section lost in her thoughts as she perused the cheeses when she thought she heard her old nickname.

"Is that Dee LaFontaine, author extraordinaire?"

This time she turned around. There was no mistaking the person in front of her. Older but still so very much the same as she remembered.

"Randy? Randy Longmont? Is that really you?"

"In the flesh, baby girl."

"I don't believe it."

"I know. Right? And on New Year's Eve! Go figure." Randy leaned in to hug her before awkwardly catching himself. "Is that okay? Mind a hug from an old lover?"

She drew her arms around his shoulders. "Of course, don't be silly." Dropping her keys, they both squatted to pick them up nearly bumping heads. "It's okay," she said. "I've got it."

They stood to an uncomfortable silence. Amanda fidgeted with her keys and gloves while Randy switched his gloves from one hand to the other.

"So," she said raising her eyebrows while watching his lips. When they were together, he had a beard. Never had she seen him up close and in-person with a goatee before.

"So," he replied undoing the knot to the gray scarf around his neck before his expression turned serious. "Hey, I'm sorry about your husband."

Amanda shot him a puzzled look.

"Read it in the papers. You know, on account of you being famous and all."

Amanda's face reddened as she nodded in acknowledgement. "Yeah, I always forget that. Thank you. How are your parents?"

It was a painful question because when she and Randy parted, Amanda not only lost Randy, but she also lost his parents too. This kept her so guarded that she refused to spend time getting to know Brett's parents beyond that of just a superficial relationship. She preferred to keep it cordial. Distant. It worked, as far as she thought. When Brett passed unexpectedly, there was no lingering relationship to keep the wound raw. Open. It was difficult enough when so many things were a constant reminder of him.

Amanda then realized it was a lot like what she went through with Randy. But Randy didn't die. When they went their separate ways, it just felt like he did.

"Mom passed a few years back," Randy replied. "Before your mom, actually."

Amanda sucked on her lower lip trying not to let the gravity of the news affect her. Though the matriarch of the Longmont family was quite protective of her son, Randy, she took a liking to Amanda. They had similar tastes. Enjoyed many of the same things. Shared the same sense of humor. Unlike memories of Amanda's aunt, who only sought to keep the spotlight on herself in nearly every engagement, milking drama whenever she could, there was never any competition between Randy's mother and herself. It didn't even matter that Amanda was so much younger. The laughs and camaraderie were real and always enjoyed. Something Amanda never experienced ever again.

Amanda exhaled loudly. "Wow. I'm sorry, Randy."

Shifting in place, Randy pressed his lips together and looked out over the store before speaking. "Appreciate that." Knowing Randy, Amanda sensed he was trying not to think about his mom, which as she was already aware, was ten times more difficult given the season.

There wasn't much else to say. And the discomfiture was growing rather than easing. Randy didn't seem to be on Facebook, so she didn't know much about his life. She didn't like looking for people anyway and kept her interactions on the social network brief. That was her guarding herself. She knew it wasn't healthy to get caught up with what others were doing.

Though she googled him a few times over the years, the only thing she learned was that he remarried. The ring on his finger indicated that was still the case.

"Your books are doing pretty well, then, huh?" The question drew her focus from his hand back to his face.

Amanda smiled. "Things are going pretty well, yeah."

An elderly gentleman shuffled by and excused himself as he walked between the former couple.

Amanda noticed Randy making a face. "What?"

Randy waved his hand as he spoke with a whisper. "I think he passed gas."

This made Amanda laugh. Then she suddenly realized they were hogging the spot in front of the cheeses. "It's probably the cheese or the sour milk from the dairy over there."

Randy wasn't convinced. He flared his nostrils and backed away. "Say what you will but he gifted us some flatulence."

"Listen to you. 'Gifted us!' Jesus, you haven't changed a bit," she said as they both moved to spot where there was less traffic.

"Still have your dogs?" Randy asked.

She shot him a puzzled *How do you know?* look. "The Internet," they both said at the same time laughing.

"I love how you've been able to keep tabs on me and I don't know anything about how you've been."

"Well, Big Shot, you shouldn't make yourself so public."

"You know what I mean. Besides, I'm not really *that* public. And I am certainly not *that* famous."

"To this area you are. To this state. And you're on Facebook," he said mockingly making quotation marks with his fingers. "Yeah, that's right. My sister keeps me informed."

Amanda felt herself flush. So smooth and effortless was Randy's delivery and timing, it was as if the years melted away and they were teenagers again. It felt good to laugh. Her face was hurting from smiling so much. But the more she realized it, the more self-conscious she became. "Oh, that's nice. So, you have your sister spying on me?"

Randy chuckled and raised his hands in defense. "Social media has turned back the clock, my dear. It's like everyone is back in high school again using that damn thing. Not sure that's a good thing, either."

"My agent tells me I am not out in the public eye *enough*. So, say what you will but I really don't put myself out there as much as you think. Just like that time shortly after we broke up when you thought I was out partying and dancing every night."

Randy seemed to wince at the recollection.

Watching Randy's reaction to the memory Amanda feared whatever good will led to this encounter had been squandered in that mere second. "Long story short I only have a social media account because of my books. It allows me to promote my events and keep up with people I meet, including my former students."

Randy acknowledged with a nod.

"My goodness, I hardly even post anything," she said embarrassed that she was dragging the subject on longer than necessary. "Who needs to know what I'm doing every minute of every day?"

Randy smirked. "Now you know why I avoid it."

"Yeah, but aren't you kind of in the same situation? It's good for you to get your work out there, no?" Randy was a caricature artist and started showing up on the Internet a few years back.

"Truth be told my wife does all that for me. I'd rather not spend too much time on there," Randy admitted as he slapped his gloves into his open hand.

"I've seen some stuff from you online, though."

"Oh, sure. I venture every now and then, but it's still not my thing. Definitely not Facebook."

"How are you doing with that?"

"With what? My wife?"

"Your art, silly."

He smiled. "Oh. Good."

"And the wife, I gather, is also good."

"She's nice. A keeper. You'd like her."

A knot twisted in Amanda's stomach. Why do people always say that? She was sure she would like his wife about as much as he would have liked Brett.

Randy removed his fedora to wipe the perspiration from his shaved head.

Amanda resisted the urge to run her hand over her ex-lover's smooth scalp. "I like the hat. It's very... you. I'm liking the whole look to be honest."

She was being serious. When she knew him, he had a full head of hair. The compliment touched Randy. He smiled broadly at her words. "You should see my wife's nieces and nephews when I show them pictures back from... you know" and he gestured knowing full well she'd understand it to mean when they were together. Laughing, he added, "And they can't get over the hair."

She laughed with him. "Ah, yes. The pompadour."

"Or the caterpillar that used to be on my upper lip!"

They both laughed heartily at that, tears in their eyes.

"Hard to believe so many years have gone by, huh?"

"Yeah," Amanda agreed. "Can't tell you how often I find myself saying those same words these days. It's not even like we're *that* old. Yet."

"You know, I began shaving my head after it started coming out in clumps."

"Oh, no. Why was that? Were you sick?"

"I was doing an art project for a client. You know, thought I could jump right into the biz. But I didn't have all the materials I needed. Even worse, I can't draw anything realistic to save my life. I worked on that project for nearly a week straight without sleep."

"Oh, my God."

"Yeah. It was around the holidays. I was staying with my parents for Christmas. On the pillow and in the shower, it was like something out of a horror movie." He accentuated the tale miming clumps of hair in his hands. "Scary."

"Wow. Yeah. Very scary. Your Dad always had a beautiful head of hair."

Randy nodded. "I know. He did. Still does, as a matter of fact."

A kid running by bumped into Randy causing him to drop his fedora. "This may be too forward," he said picking up the hat and placing it back onto his head, "and I know it's late..."

Amanda glanced at her watch. "Yeah, five is sooo late."

"Well, this old guy is usually beginning to wind down for the evening around this time. Doesn't matter that it is New Year's."

"Guess you really have aged."

"Ouch. Don't tell me you don't have a routine in place. It comes with the age bracket."

Amanda ignored the valid point about the routine. He was correct of course. "Anyway, you were saying?"

"Yeah, I was just gonna ask you if you wanted to get a drink. Or coffee."

She eyed him suspiciously for a moment.

"Hey, I won't be offended if you say no. I mean, what are the odds of us bumping into each other? Here. At this time of year."

"What *are you doing* in this area?" Amanda asked.

"My wife's parents live in the area."

"I see."

"But…"

"But what?"

"There was a little family drama. Thought it best to get some fresh air."

Amanda couldn't help but belch out a laugh. "Oh, my God. I am so sorry. I didn't mean to… I am sorry to hear."

"Happens in all families, right?" Randy said cocking his head and widening his eyes until Amanda laughed. "Seriously, though, I thought age was supposed to change that. Did it for you? It's like people don't change. At all."

"It did for me because my husband was a very calm man. We both never gave into the drama. When forced to, I was... I am of a different mindset from before. When we were together. But when I was a kid, I was the rebellious daughter. Never acted like a proper girl. Tomboy all the way. You know that. And all the arguments with my parents. But leaving the family for a decade helped a bit."

"Well, that will never happen with Tina. So..."

"So, I guess I'll just leave you to finish your shopping then."

"Whoa. Just like that?"

"What?"

"Well, you did seem agreeable to getting a coffee or something?"

"Yeah, but you said—"

"I didn't rescind the offer, did I?"

"Well, no, but I..."

"Hey, it's cool. It's Christmas and we haven't seen each other for a long time. It'll be nice. We'll make it quick."

"Really?" she asked. She couldn't believe her ears.

"Yeah," he said softly, jutting out his elbow. "Shall I walk you to your car."

* * *

"A toast," he said after unsuccessfully uncorking the bottle with a Swiss Army knife. Part of the cork had to be pushed into the bottle to clear the neck.

"Who'd have thought it would be so much trouble to remove a cork?" Amanda remarked.

"C'mon, it's always been that way," Randy said as he tossed the remaining coffee out the window from the styrofoam cup he had in the center console. "Murphy's Law. Especially when you're roughing it like we are. Pardon the leftover from this morning," he said as he poured the Merlot.

"Thank you," she said taking the cup. "Cheers."

"Cheers," he returned as they touched bottle to cup. After swallowing a sip, he turned to Amanda. "Not bad."

Amanda laughed. "Then why the face?"

"Because it's... not bad. Cheap, but not bad."

"Prefer something else, do you?"

"For red, Merlot was my go-to years ago. These days I like Pinot Noir."

"I'm still partial to Zinfandel myself."

"Blech!" Randy scrunched up his nose. "Really? Still?"

"Yeah."

"You do know that Zin is so 1980s, right?"

"Quite the sommelier these days, are we? At least I'm not drinking Lambrusco like you and my dad did. What is that, by the way? Alcoholic grape juice?"

"Hey, now. I was young and inexperienced at the time."

"Mmm."

"Maybe we should have gotten champagne."

"If we had this much trouble with a bottle of wine, just imagine the trouble with a champagne cork."

"Pfft. Easy peasy."

"Yeah, we'd be here watching the clock strike midnight because you'd still be trying to remove the cork."

Randy shook his head. "That wouldn't be so bad now, would it?"

Amanda ignored Randy's statement. "I don't know if you've seen them, but I use these grippers I got on Amazon now for everything."

"Me, too," Randy said with a grin. "Hell of a lot better."

"I know. Anyone can open a bottle now."

"Wow, the snow is really coming down," Randy observed from the driver's seat of his truck as the two watched the flakes pile up on the front windshield. He turned the ignition key to the 'on' position to defrost the windows and pump in a little bit of heat. When the blowing air wasn't warming, he started the vehicle.

"I don't remember what the forecast was for tonight."

"Thought we were getting a snow squall, but temps are supposed to warm up. Something about a front."

"Interesting. So, what's Tina like?"

Randy spun his head in Amanda's direction. He was about to ask her how far she lived from the store. "Just like that, huh? No transition? Just cut to the chase."

Amanda chuckled. "Must be the wine."

"Still a lightweight, I see."

Amanda smiled. "If you only knew. So... what is she like?"

Randy made a face. "Why, Mrs. LaFontaine, if I didn't know you any better, I'd swear you were flirting."

Even in the shadows, because the lot was so lit up, they could see each other clearly enough. Engaged in an unplanned visit after two decades with the man who was essentially her first husband, Amanda was happy for some cover. Dressed in comfortable clothes for lounging around the house, she wasn't dressed for socializing. She didn't do her hair before leaving the house. She had no makeup on. No perfume on. She couldn't remember when the last day was this week that she shaved her legs. It didn't matter. She wasn't going anywhere. But she nearly had a panic attack trying to remember if she brushed her teeth this morning. She made every effort to block the vain thoughts from her mind since Randy already saw her in all her aged glory in the brightly lit grocery store. If there was ever a time for flirting this was not it.

"Careful, Randy," Amanda warned, clicking her tongue. "There's flirting and there's being playful. I'm curious about the woman in your life is all. Besides, I'm not feeling nor looking very glamorous. And you, sir, are married."

"Really?" he asked lowering his voice. "That's not the way I see it. I see the same beautiful girl I knew from high school. The one who flirted with me in Art class. My high school sweetheart."

"You sure you haven't had too much wine?" If she were younger maybe she might be flattered. But she also knew Randy. At their age, after all these years, his compliments seemed forced. Disingenuous. Still, the laughs came easily. There was no denying the warmth she felt recalling these early days of first love. First kisses. "If I recall, your flirting in Art got us — no, got me — in trouble."

"Did it now?"

Amanda rolled her eyes. "You don't remember?"

Randy shook his head smiling. "No. What happened?"

"I don't believe this. I was spoken to after class. Me! I never said 'boo' in there. She didn't believe me, either, when I told her you were the one talking. The one making me laugh."

Randy laughed heartily. "I think I need more wine," he said before taking another swig. He offered to fill her cup, but she put up a hand.

"In a little bit," she said before needling him a bit more. "Well? Why so coy about Tina?"

"Okay, I'll give. Tina's... great."

"That's it? Just great?"

"What? What else do you want me to say? Yeah, she's great."

"But?"

"But nothing. No buts."

"Well, why don't you want to tell me more about her. Is it because of the drama going on?"

Randy shrugged. "Maybe a little of that and maybe it's because I'm hanging out with the first person I fell in love with and I don't want to talk about much else right now that would spoil the moment."

Amanda studied Randy's face. Even in the limited light she saw a look of melancholy and placed a hand to his cheek. "Okay. Fair enough. I'm sorry."

Randy brought up his hand and placed it over hers. "Tell me about your husband. Were you happy?"

His hand on hers was warm. She stroked his cheek with her thumb before withdrawing her hand, avoiding his attempt to hold it. "He was a good man. A kind man. Grateful. Gentle. Died much too young."

They were both facing each other. Randy moved some hair from her eyes. "Are you happy?"

"Are *you* happy?"

"You know my mother adored you. No, she didn't just adore you, she loved you. She never stopped talking about you. Used to piss Tina off like you wouldn't believe. Even years after you... Even in her final days..."

Amanda pressed her lips together at Randy's admission. "Guess it's a good thing we never actually got married then. Don't they like Tina?"

"They think the world of Tina. My mom just really took the breakup hard. Took what you did hard... because she enjoyed having you around so much. It was never the same with Tina. Now Tina feels guilty she didn't spend enough time getting to know my mother before she died."

Amanda loved Randy's family, especially his mom. But when things got rocky, she came to the defense of her son. As it should be. Amanda didn't fault anyone for it. To her, it was just another example of how she didn't have anyone to rely on back then. Before she grew strong enough to be independent. To stand on her own without needing the approval of her family. Or a man.

"You know, they made every effort to help you — us — out. Your family situation was not your fault. That you wanted to do more with your life was not your fault. What you did after was." There was no mistaking the pain in Randy's tone. The memory of the past was difficult to revisit, no matter how many years may have gone by.

"I remember catching sight of you three at the kitchen table. Saw you through the crack of the door. Looking happy. Laughing. Something we hadn't done in a long while." Amanda shrugged. "I saw no other solution. You guys were better off without me."

"Holy shit, Dee! You tried to kill yourself!"

It was something they never talked about because following her inpatient treatment at the local hospital's psychiatric unit, she was kicked out of the house.

Hospitalized for ten days, there was no communication. No visits. Even when she was allowed to make calls and tried reaching Randy, no one picked up. No one called back.

Inside she was trapped watching fellow inpatients vomit into their plates during mealtime and shuffle about as medicated zombies. She slept in a room with no doors. There was no privacy. Even when using the bathroom.

Aside from group sessions and self-reflection activities, counselors maintained a cool detachment. There were no engaging conversations. Conversations with others was discouraged. Anything said aloud was scrutinized. Recorded.

During her hospitalization Amanda wanted to believe in the system and was ready to bare her soul. Fears and all. But when her psychiatrist repeatedly disregarded what she did share and instead told her what her problem was without listening, she knew it was up to her to make things right again. To make herself whole. In her most vulnerable moment, she was denied a voice. She swore that would never happen again.

Eschewing any kind of medication, Amanda even entertained outpatient support services but since they were only available when she was working it only emboldened her more. The universe may have been against her and the road to recovery long and winding, but it only fueled her with a renewed sense of purpose.

Once discharged, she never saw Randy again and Randy's parents wouldn't let her back in the house. They left her car at the hospital and the keys with the front desk. Her father was insistent that she not set foot in their home ever again. He even went so far as to have all of Amanda's stuff left in the driveway. Amanda was given one day to have it removed because Randy's old man was all set to haul anything remaining off to the dump.

Amanda took the bottle from Randy and downed more wine. Without the cup. "You've no idea what I went through when I got out. It was like starting over. But at the very bottom."

Randy said nothing.

"And please, tell me what choice did I have? I would have been stuck becoming a schoolmarm getting paid the salary of a babysitter. We lived out in the boonies, Randy. My God, there were lucrative job opportunities I couldn't have dreamed possible for a woman in various parts of the state. We could have bought a house with what I made after leaving. Instead, had everything worked out between us, we'd STILL be living with your parents because we still wouldn't be able to afford anything."

"That's no reason for you to try to kill yourself. We could have moved."

"You know that's not true. We couldn't afford to." She tossed her hair back from her shoulders feeling slightly annoyed. "Why does any of this still matter to you? It's been twenty years."

"Yeah, but—no"

"Yeah, but nothing. I'm not the pushover I was when we were together."

"That hurts!"

"Well, it's true."

"For the record, I didn't think you were a pushover. But who and what you were before... those qualities... were attractive."

"What? Being helpless? Dependent? Glad you now approve. Seems to me at the end you were complaining about it."

"That's 'cause you were freakin' hot and cold at the time."

"Maybe. But you were depressed all the time."

"Oh, come on. I was itching to start an art career. I finished school a year ahead of you and had nothing to show for it. Then after you graduated you were teaching at places that didn't pay well."

"That's a rural teacher's salary for you, Randy. But you wouldn't agree to leave Mommy long enough for us to move where we could have earned better wages."

"Well, I just felt like all I did was work. I was going crazy working to bring in more money for us. But the jobs were shit jobs!"

"You were going crazy? You stopped making love to me. You were always yelling, making me feel like I didn't exist. You spent hours talking to people on that damn AOL account. It was like you resented me for trying to grow as a person. As a professional. Because I wasn't the dutiful wife your mom was to your dad."

"Wow, who are you?

"What, the truth hurt?"

"Out of context, none of what you are saying is accurate."

"Mmm. Still in denial then, huh?"

Randy put up his hands. "Fine. You know what? You win. I'll obviously never be able to defend or explain myself."

"You just don't want to take any responsibility for your side of it, that's all."

"It was a very tough time, okay. I was confused. I was upset. I was angry. Is that what you want to hear?"

"At what? From what I remember your anger was always directed at me. Tell me it wasn't. You resented me for things not going the way you planned."

"We planned," Randy tried to clarify.

"No, the way you planned."

"I was an art major with a useless degree. I wasn't contributing. I was supposed to be the man of the house."

"Dammit, Randy. Your degree was worth plenty. You weren't making anything because you lived in the freaking sticks."

Randy picked at a piece of rubber on the steering wheel. "It just sucked, that's all. At one point I honestly didn't know if you had gone gay on me."

"What did you just say?"

Randy looked at Amanda with puppy dog eyes. "You heard me."

"You're lucky I don't belt you."

"See! Who... What woman says that to a man? You were a bit butch there for a while."

"You do realize how offensive you're being."

"Just speaking truth."

Amanda reached out to the middle console to turn off the heat before flipping the switch on her door to drop her window. Randy flinched unsure of what she was about to do.

"Chill out, Sally. It's too hot and I need some air."

"Okay. Okay," he said as he turned off the ignition.

After letting the snowy cool air blow about her face for a few moments, she brought the window back up while talking. "I figured once I graduated college everything was going to change, you know. I mean, we were doing everything right. Or so I thought. You graduated. Then I graduated. My God, after suffering the low salary at the Catholic school, I got a public position. Seems we had a foot in the door and then after a year I was reduced to part-time."

Amanda wiped at something on her face that Randy couldn't see before continuing. "Tried to hang in there for the year thinking it's only temporary only to lose it all because of budget cuts. Then, if that wasn't humiliating enough, I was working in a factory to make up for what you couldn't provide." She turned to him. "You want to talk butch, you should have seen some of the women who worked third shift."

Randy smirked.

"You were supposed to be my partner, Randy. But you couldn't handle your jobs without always having some kind of breakdown. And you had support. I never did. Yeah, we had no money. That's no kind of life but we were together. Both just starting out.

We were supposed to be a team. Supporting each other."

"Yeah, I don't miss that part at all."

"Being a team?"

"No, not having any money."

"At least now you're an artist involved with the community. Had I remained, I would have never known that there's another world out there. Between the ridiculously low pay and job scarcity in the area at the time, I would have probably never found the time to write while working other jobs. And let's face it, you would have never become the artist you are today."

"Whatever," Randy whispered as he looked out his side window. "You still would have divorced me."

"I don't know. I just know you wouldn't' have been able to deal with being far away from your mother."

"There were reasons."

"Oh?"

"They aren't important now."

"Well, you know what I've been saying is true."

"See, now that's like the old Amanda I remember. Unlike you, my wife understands me."

"Sounds like it. Is that why there's drama, then? Is that why you've been in such a rush to get home?"

At that point Amanda gathered up her keys and gloves. The bottle of wine empty, they had clearly run out of things to say. She threw her coat over her arms. "I guess that's it," she said as she pulled the door handle.

Randy put his hand on her arm. She glanced back waiting for him to say something. Anything. Instead, he awkwardly pulled her to him. Holding her face in his hands, he kissed her.

Feeling violated, she shoved him hard. "The fuck, Randy!"

"Why?" he asked again, his expression full of anguish. "Why did you try to kill yourself? Goddammit, Mandy. You may not have succeeded but I swear you..." Randy gulped hard. "You sure did a job on all of us. You may not have died that night but a part of us did."

Amanda hopped out and slammed the door behind her. With long angry strides, she started back to her car before she stopped nearly slipping on the slick pavement.

Coming around to the driver's side of Randy's truck, she held on to the side view mirror for support and stepped up on the running board. Powering down the window, Randy greeted her with wet eyes. As Amanda put a hand on his cheek, he closed his eyes but dared not move.

Leaning in, she whispered in his ear that she was happy. "Now *you* need to find your happiness." Before withdrawing, she gently kissed his cheek. "Take care, Randy."

Randy was silent as he watched his first love make her way through the dark parking lot and once more out of his life.

Amanda reached her car at the same time she heard Randy's truck start up and drive off. Seeing her silhouette in the driver's side window transported her back to her high school days. Brought back an old familiar pain.

As the snow turned into rain, she climbed behind the wheel to make her way back home.

www.ingramcontent.com/pod-product-compliance
Lightning Source LLC
Chambersburg PA
CBHW070753120626
46557CB00002B/576